EARTHQUAKE AT DAWN

Kristiana Gregory

GULLIVER BOOKS
HARCOURT BRACE & COMPANY
SAN DIEGO   NEW YORK   LONDON

Requests for permission to make copies of any part of the work should be
mailed to: Permissions Department, Harcourt Brace & Company,
6277 Sea Harbor Drive, Orlando, Florida 32887-6777.

Permission to print excerpts of a letter by Mary Exa Atkins Campbell
was granted by James Atkins Tarver and Evelyn Tarver.
Permission to print Edith Irvine's photographs was granted by
Brigham Young University Photo Archives.

Library of Congress Cataloging-in-Publication Data
Gregory, Kristiana.
Earthquake at dawn/by Kristiana Gregory. — 1st ed.
p.   cm. — (Great episodes)
Includes excerpts of a letter by Mary Exa Atkins Campbell.
Includes bibliographical references.
Summary: A novelization of twenty-two-year-old photographer Edith Irvine's
experiences in the aftermath of the 1906 San Francisco earthquake, as seen
through the eyes of fifteen-year-old Daisy, a fictitious traveling companion.
ISBN 0-15-200446-7
1. Irvine, Edith — Juvenile fiction.   [1. Irvine, Edith — Fiction.
2. Earthquakes — California — San Francisco — Fiction.   3. San Francisco
(Calif.) — Fiction.   4. Photography — Fiction.]   I. Campbell, Mary Exa
Atkins.   II. Title.   III. Series.
PZ7.G8619Ear   1992
[Fic] — dc20   92-715

Designed by Lisa Peters
Printed in the United States of America
C D E F G

EARTHQUAKE
AT DAWN

Edith Irvine
Courtesy of Brigham Young University Photo Archives

For our sons,

Greg and Cody

I believe that there is more danger to be apprehended from the concealment of facts, or the tacit silence of public press on the topic [of earthquakes in San Francisco], than in free and open discussion of the subject and speculation for the future.
—BRET HARTE, JOURNALIST, 1866

[M]y first earthquake . . . was one which was long called the "great" earthquake; . . . The ground seemed to roll under me in waves, interrupted by a violent joggling up and down. . . . I fell up against the frame house and hurt my elbow. . . . The plastering that fell from ceilings in San Francisco that day [October 8, 1865] would have covered several acres of ground.
—MARK TWAIN, AUTHOR, 1872

Notes

IN THE EARLY MORNING of April 18, 1906, San Francisco, California, was struck by an earthquake that on today's Richter scale would have registered 8.3. At the time, officials reported the death toll at under 500, but ongoing research now estimates that fatalities exceeded 3,000.

Edith Irvine, a twenty-two-year-old photographer, was visiting San Francisco that morning. Family lore says that she had traveled from Stockton to San Francisco to begin a trip that would take her around the world, and that she was aboard a small boat in the harbor when the quake struck. After disembarking, she hid her cameras in an abandoned baby buggy. For several days she wandered among the ruins taking pictures, defying the orders of city officials who wanted to conceal the full extent of the damage.

Another Irvine legend is that Edith was on her way to San Francisco with her father to help him in a court battle involving their mines in the Mother Lode country. I have combined these two possibilities and introduced a fictional narrator: fifteen-year-old Daisy Valentine. She could easily have been one of the domestic helpers in the wealthy Irvine family.

I have woven their story around Edith's actual photographs as well as a thirty-two-page letter written by survivor Mary Exa Atkins Campbell, in which Mary Exa details her experience in the quake and subsequent fires.

Each chapter of *Earthquake at Dawn* begins with an excerpt from her letter.

The result is a work of historical fiction. For instance, both Jack London and John Barrymore later wrote about their days among the ruins, but whether or not they or Mary Exa actually met Edith is unknown. Enrico Caruso, who at the time was the world's most famous tenor, had performed with the Metropolitan Opera only hours before the first deadly tremor. Legend says that when his boat finally sailed out of the harbor, he shook his fist at the smoldering city and vowed he would never return to San Francisco.

Edith's uncle, John B. Reddick, was California's Lieutenant Governor from 1890 to 1894. In 1864 one of her great-uncles, James Irvine, purchased 108,000 acres from Spanish land grants in Southern California. The Irvine Ranch was noted for cattle, sheep, lima beans, olives, and fragrant orange groves that stretched miles across what is now Orange County. Today the City of Irvine has more than 100,000 residents.

Edith's photographs and her camera equipment are housed at the Brigham Young University library in Provo, Utah.

Kristiana Gregory
Redlands, California, 1992

Acknowledgments

I'M GRATEFUL TO my orthodontist, Dr. Roland Neufeld, and his racks of interesting magazines—specifically a *National Geographic* with an article about Edith Irvine. It would not have been possible to complete this book without Wilma Marie "Billy" Plunket, whose master's thesis on Edith and her photography taught me much; nor without Evelyn and James Atkins Tarver, who trusted me with Mary Exa's 1906 letter and indulged me with long telephone conversations.

Research was made easier with the help of Calaveras County archivist Lorrayne Kennedy, Drs. Caron and George Christison, Richard and Susi Watson, Kathryn Judd, Barbara Wyckoff McConnell at *National Geographic,* Joycelyn Mitchell at Redlands's A. K. Smiley Public Library, and Kip Rutty, photographer and terrific husband.

Most of all, for Irvine family history and anecdotes, I'm indebted to James Hayes Irvine, Edith's nephew.

*There have been any number of faint earthquake shocks
since I came here [in 1904] and a few real heavy ones, so I have never
felt quite safe and always lived in a state of uncertainty. . . . Many
people here claim to have had warnings and many suffered from spells of
'blues,' restlessness, despondency, and discontentment.*

Chapter 1

WITH OUTSTRETCHED ARMS, I carried the chamber pot across the yard to the outhouse. Holding my breath, I poured the stink through the hole in the wooden seat. Of all my duties for the Irvines, this was the worst.

I rinsed the pot at the pump, then dried my hands on my apron, careful not to step in the puddle.

How I wished I could toss the contents out the bedroom window instead of bringing the pot downstairs, for I was terrified I might spill it on one of the thick Oriental carpets. But Mrs. Irvine had a spying eye and words to remind me I no longer lived in a mining camp. There were some things civilized folks just don't do, she was fond of saying.

The screen door banged behind me as I hurried through the kitchen, which was still warm from breakfast. I grabbed a biscuit from the back of the broad iron stove, hid it in my pocket, then hurried upstairs.

"Daisy!" fumed Mrs. Irvine when I entered Edith's room. "That is the fifth time this morning you have slammed the back door, thrice you've slammed the front door. This is not a saloon." She stood in front of an open steamer trunk, a partially folded shawl draped over her arm. Her foot tapped impatiently. I slid the chamber pot under the commode, then faced her.

She was a handsome woman, tall and confident as a queen. Her waist was pinched thin by the corset I'd helped her lace that morning. I studied the small ivory buttons adorning the lace at her throat, her pearl earrings, her stern jaw. My eyes met hers.

"Yes, ma'am," I finally said.

"Very well. If we're to finish packing by tonight you'll have to move faster than that. When you and Edith board the stage tomorrow morning I want you to look like ladies, not some common . . . Oh, where is she anyway? She was supposed to be up here helping an hour ago. Go see, will you, Daisy."

I nearly skipped along the road, it felt so good to be outside on this cool morning and away from Mrs. Irvine. Through the pasture ahead I could see Edith walking along the stream, a small box camera under one arm and a tripod under the other. Her red hair hung loose down her back, and she was not only barefoot under her long skirt but comfortably without a corset as well. Her face broke into a smile when she saw me.

"Time to pack?" she called, heading my way. "Oh, Daisy, I'm so impatient, aren't you? Have you eaten yet? We have just twenty-four hours to do everything . . . *everything!*"

Edith walked briskly, and when she reached the road several wild hens that had been roosting on the fence scattered out of her way. To keep pace with her I lengthened my stride and hiked up my skirt. Often I accompanied Edith to town this way, and by the time we reached Hornbuckle's Merchandise I would be out of breath, perspiring in an unladylike manner.

Our errands were usually unnecessary, most often meant to satisfy Edith's curiosity. A stroll into a shop often meant overhearing an interesting conversation or becoming part of one. As I was her family's servant, folks granted me polite nods, nothing more. It was Edith who had their respect.

She was Mokelumne Hill's schoolteacher, an honored position in California's Mother Lode. Her pupils were the children of a laundrywoman, a seamstress, miners, ranchers, saloon keepers, and other rough characters.

Now as we walked along the rutted road toward the house I felt a rush of happiness. This was my last day of obeying Mrs. Irvine's orders and the last day I would clean someone else's chamber pot. The roses below the porch smelled sweeter than ever, their fragrant clusters of pink and yellow in early bloom.

Edith dropped her tripod into the umbrella stand, then carried her camera upstairs. Lee Ha Sing was easing a trunk down the attic steps. His blue cotton smock hung to his knees over matching trousers. He smiled and bowed when we met on the landing.

"Good morning, Charlie," said Edith. "Daisy, could you help here while I see what Mother's doing?"

The next three hours saw a flurry of activity as petticoats, skirts, linen blouses, stockings, bloomers, and fitted wool coats were folded, packed, then re-packed. Dozens of photographic glass plates, along with Edith's prints of Yosemite, were carefully laid between the layers of clothes in one of the trunks.

Charlie brought several carpetbags down from the attic. We tucked Edith's cameras and more plates into two of these, making them so heavy I didn't know how either of us would carry them. Our tickets, with maps and an itinerary, were in a third bag; our hairbrushes, nightgowns, toiletries, and a few *Collier's* magazines were in a fourth.

Mrs. Irvine was a solemn overseer. She penciled each item into a ledger, underlining twice the things I was borrowing. Only after thinking for many long moments did she agree I could take two books: *Call of the Wild* and *Kim*. These volumes were "lit-ra-choor," not the dime novels favored by—here she cleared her throat—"riffraff."

"Mother," said Edith, trying not to laugh, "Daisy can read as well as I. She had the best teacher in gold country, don't forget."

"Fiddlesticks. Let's go over your maps again. I want to make sure you girls have committed them to memory."

I sat atop a trunk squeezed between the bureau and the brass bed. A breeze stirred the lace curtains, and I could hear woodpeckers rattling against the mulberry tree outside. Bad Boy, my large gray cat, moseyed over from his perch by the window and curled up on my lap, purring loudly. My mind drifted while Edith recited every port, train depot, and capital city—details that would take us around the world in fourteen months.

There would be a stage production in Melbourne, Australia; an opera in London; museums in Vienna and Copenhagen; a Mozart festival in Salzburg; travel cross the isthmus of Panama by mule and canoe. Dates and places blurred together, but not Edith's main reason for going: the International Photographic Society had invited her to Paris to exhibit the prints she'd taken of Yosemite National Park. The very mention of this prestigious event made Mrs. Irvine breathless. It was an honor for the Irvines, who, two generations before, had been immigrants from Ireland.

Edith was an internationally respected photographer and I, Daisy Valentine, was to be her trust-worthy assistant.

The moment I was most excited about was still two days away. At one o'clock in the afternoon, Wednesday, April 18, 1906, we would sail out of San Francisco Bay aboard the SS *Susanna,* bound for Australia via the Sandwich Islands and Fiji. Finally, despite new duties, I would be living my dream: ever since my childhood in Miners' Gulch, I had wanted to explore foreign cities and to hear languages different from my own.

he moment I felt the house tremble and the plaster and bric-a-brac begin to fall, I leaped out of bed and rushed out to the front door, which I had a time unbolting on account of shifting of house, and while trying to get it opened I was bumped back and forth against it until I was sure the house would fall before I got out. It rocked like a ship on rough seas.

Chapter 2

AN HOUR BEFORE SUNRISE, we arrived at Moke-lumne Hill's depot, a large tiled room on the first floor of the Leger Hotel, dimly lit by gas lamps. While we waited for the stagecoach, well-wishers filed in to say good-bye. I sat alone near a window. The tearful embraces were for Edith. Every few moments she cast a sympathetic eye my way, as if to say, Hold on, Daisy, we'll be leaving soon.

Charlie served hot coffee from the little stove he'd set up outside. His brother, Johnny Lee Sing, scooped cinnamon rolls dripping with frosting from a cast-iron pan. The crowd was festive except for two people who were struggling to keep their composure: Mrs. Irvine and Dr. Roland Willy.

Dr. Willy was the town's only physician, a quiet, gentle man who long ago had set adoring eyes on our schoolteacher. During the past year, on our many excursions to Hornbuckle's Merchandise, I had observed him hurrying from his office for a "chance" encounter with Edith.

Every time he asked her to accompany him to the river for a picnic or to Watson's Café for supper, she gave elaborate excuses, most of which involved her camera or her need to study. Mrs. Irvine was puzzled as to why her daughter refused to be courted by the good doctor. He had money, social standing, and the pleasant courtesies of a properly educated man. At twenty-two years of age, Edith was in danger of becoming an old maid.

This did not worry me. I knew Edith's curiosity was what made her a good photographer and a good teacher. If she settled down now, she'd miss her chance to see the world and, perhaps, would not be recognized for her art. Her refusals made perfect sense to me. I wished I could explain this to her mother and to Dr. Willy, but a servant's opinion is rarely asked for and I did not want to be called uppity for offering it.

Dr. Willy held his derby in front of him. His hair was parted slickly down the middle and there was the beginning of a mustache on his upper lip. He appeared nervous as he stood next to Edith, and every time he tried to talk someone interrupted.

Small gifts were being pressed into Edith's arms, as if she were a bride on her wedding day. Her brother, Bob, gave her a pair of binoculars tiny enough to fit in her palm, and Mr. Peek, the postmaster, gave her some envelopes. As Mr. and Mrs. Hornbuckle handed her a flat tin of mints, they cast disapproving looks at me. A young teacher traveling the globe with an even younger companion—both unmarried—was a prospect that flustered the citizens of this small town.

Six older, respectable women had applied for the position of Edith's chaperone. One by one they had come to the house to answer Mr. Irvine's questions and to chat politely with Mrs. Irvine. Yes, they said proudly, they were in good health, although two leaned on canes and later the others admitted to a little rheumatism. One afternoon when I rolled the tea tray into the parlor and blurted out how I'd like to see the Eiffel Tower, Edith's eyes lit up and she turned to her parents.

"I've reached my decision. Daisy will be my escort."

Mrs. Irvine's gasp was so loud that Charlie rushed in from the kitchen to see what was wrong. I stood in delighted silence.

"Daisy's not afraid of bugs, she's not flatulent, nor does she snore," explained Edith. "She walks energetically and she knows the difference between a telephoto and a telephone. I don't know why I didn't consider her in the first place."

And so it was settled. But folks in town pointed out that I was only fifteen years old and also that I'd been raised in a mining camp with no suitable feminine influence. This worried Mrs. Irvine. My lack of culture was sure to degrade her daughter. Edith had no such doubts.

Now that we were packed and the team of horses was hitched to the stage outside, my heart lifted. In the gray morning light Mrs. Irvine embraced Edith one last time, then unpinned her hat and set it on her daughter's head.

"If you won't put your hair up at least you can wear a hat. All proper ladies and gentlemen do," she said.

We settled into the dusty coach, facing each other knee to knee. Mr. Irvine would escort us as far as San Francisco, where he had a meeting at City Hall the next morning.

"Good-bye, good-bye!" came the cries as the driver pulled himself up to his seat. Just as he snapped the reins, Dr. Willy rushed up to the opened flap and gave Edith the rose he'd been holding.

"I'll miss you!" he managed to call above the jangling of harnesses.

The thrill of leaving was almost more than I could bear. I wanted to erupt with giggles or bounce on the prickly seat. Edith sat next to her father. He stroked her hand tenderly.

"Well, darling," he said to her, "how does it feel to be finally starting your grand adventure? I know you and Daisy will have a wonderful time and that you'll both look after each other."

"I'll miss you, Papa," she answered. There was a sparkle in Edith's eye and her face kept breaking into a grin. Our heavy linen skirts hid our restless feet. When she kicked my shoe and I kicked her back, we laughed out loud like schoolgirls.

Smiling, Mr. Irvine shook his head and laughed. "The world had better watch out for you two."

By late afternoon we had descended the winding, parched hills into Stockton, a city with electric street lamps and a few horseless carriages. At the Sacramento River port, our trunks and bags were transferred to the squat packetboat *Maria*. Soon we were motoring away from the dock, westward, between high, grassy banks.

Our picnic supper, so carefully prepared that morning by Charlie, was a delicious assortment of meats, pickles, cheeses, and plump, juicy oranges. We ate aboard, sitting among clusters of luggage and rope.

"Papa, do you think there'll be storms at sea? Australia is so far away." Edith was gazing at the vast yellow ranchlands that met the sky. Her head rested against her father's shoulder.

"I suspect there will be storms, my dear," he answered after a moment. "But there also will be exquisite sunsets that will take your breath away; that, I can assure you."

"Papa, what happens when you get to City Hall?"

Edith changed the subject in the easy manner she had with her father. They often spent evenings like this in the parlor, exchanging ideas and opinions, never in a logical manner that I could follow.

"First thing," he said, "is to make legal copies of our certificates and documents. That's where proof of Irvine ownership is."

"But what if someone has beaten you to it and forged your signature, Papa? What then?"

Mr. Irvine's voice was soft. "Our family could lose everything, my dear. Everything."

I knew they were talking about the threat of claim jumpers taking over their gold quartz mines and other business ventures in the Mother Lode. After a while Mr. Irvine excused himself with a tip of his hat.

As dusk fell, gas lamps flickered on and passengers began wandering around deck in the cool breeze. Edith unpinned her mother's wide-brimmed hat. It was ivory with a blue velvet ribbon around the crown. Before I could stop her, she leaned over the rail and sailed it into the churning wake. In an instant the hat filled with water and disappeared.

"It was a stupid old hat," Edith said, "the same one Mother's been trying to get me to wear since I was sixteen. It was . . ." Edith stopped when she saw the expression on my face. "Why, Daisy, would you have worn it? I'm sorry. . . . I just didn't think."

I lifted my chin and turned away. Now that I'd learned how to coil and pouf my hair on top of my head, a hat would have made me look like a real lady. Her stupid old hat could have been *my* hat. Below us, water swished along the hull, the only sign we were moving through the darkness. The deck vibrated with the chugging engine.

"Daisy, it's just that mothers can be so irksome. Mine isn't called 'Boss Lady' for nothing."

"At least you *have* a mother."

For a long while we sat on a smooth mahogany bench, Edith's shawl tucked over our laps. I couldn't stay mad at her. I knew she hadn't meant to upset me.

The night seemed strangely busy with barking and howling farm dogs, as if the moon were full, but there was no moon at all. Stars shimmered in the cold sky.

When the captain rang his midnight bell, Edith and I curled next to each other on deck, protected from the wind by our trunks and one blanket pulled to our chins. Mr. Irvine sat watchful at our feet. It would be another five hours before the river floated us into San Pablo Bay.

Edith shook me awake. "We're here," she cried. "Look how huge the city is. Look!"

The wind had died down, but it was still cold and damp on deck. I did not want to leave the warmth of our blanket. Edith pointed to the east, where the sky was turning a light, clear blue. It was already dawn. Had I slept so long?

"Berkeley's over there. That's where I finished school. And there, at the bottom of Telegraph Hill, is the Barbary Coast. You don't go there unless you're doing things you're not supposed to."

"Yuh," said Mr. Irvine, yawning. He stretched his arms, then combed his fingers through his graying hair before putting on his hat. "Many a poor fellow has been shanghaied after a drink too many with the wrong kind of gal. The Barbary is a cesspool, no doubt about it."

A church bell somewhere in the city pealed five times. "That's the tower bell at Saint Mary's," Edith said. "We'll be docking soon. It's five o'clock. *Five o'clock.*" She threw her head back in delight and looped her arm through mine. "Eight more hours, Daisy, and we leave for Australia. You and I, partners all the way!"

Still sleepy and enjoying Edith's enthusiasm, I said

nothing. When she threw herself, laughing, into her father's arms, he lifted his face to the sky and held her.

"I'm going to miss my little girl," he said.

"Papa."

He chuckled. "All right, all right. You'll be back before Mother and I know it. We're excited for you, sweetheart, we really are. It's just going to be . . . a little quieter, that's all." Seeing that I was now standing, he opened an arm for me. "You, too, Daisy. I'll miss you, too."

Together we leaned against the railing. I held the blanket over my shoulders against the chill. A wonderful new smell filled my lungs. Salt air. We were almost touching the Pacific Ocean. I could see the dark outlines of fishing boats, their red and green running lights moving with the swells as they headed seaward. A rocky island loomed ahead in the bay. Lights atop high walls made me think it must be Alcatraz, where villains like Slippery Jim Pete get locked up.

As we neared the city, we could hear isolated clangs of a trolley. Streetlamps dotting the hills began to dim, and a few minutes after five o'clock, they blinked out. Now the only lights were those glowing from kitchen windows and doorways.

From the Barbary Coast came the tinkling of a piano, also laughter. The sound of a cow mooing carried across the water so clearly, I thought for a moment the cow was aboard. It was drowned out by an eruption of barking dogs and whinnying horses, sounds so startling that Edith and I looked at each other.

At that instant something thumped our boat. Edith and I grabbed the rail. Mr. Irvine hugged Edith protectively and looked beyond the bow.

"What was that, Papa? Did we hit something?" she asked. We all looked up at the captain, who had stepped out to the upper deck, searching the waters.

"See anything?" he called to his crew.

Before anyone could answer, we heard an ear-splitting boom, as if ten cannons had exploded. All heads turned toward shore. Immediately every light blacked out, darkening the city into a silhouette against the lightening sky.

"Papa, what's happened?"

A woman next to us screamed, then someone cried out the horrible word:

"Earthquake!"

*Streams of people in white and colored garments
poured into the streets and for a time there we remained, a mourning,
groaning, sobbing, wailing, weeping and praying crowd. The most
pathetic of all were the poor half-clad women clasping little
infants in their arms and begging for mercy.*

Chapter 3

BEFORE OUR EYES, in the dim light of dawn, we watched pillars of dust rise from the waking city. We could see wharves crumble. A shanty fell onto a three-masted barkentine, causing it to roll onto its side. As the ship began to sink, a nearby dock loaded with coal caved into the water. The harbor was a forest of masts swaying as if on high seas.

Many of us screamed in terror. Houses rode the bucking streets as if playing crack-the-whip. Everywhere, buildings tumbled. Church bells clanged wildly. The loudest noise was a rumble deep inside the earth. It made me think of a locomotive passing at full speed.

Mr. Irvine checked his pocket watch nervously. "Five-thirteen A.M. I wonder what the captain plans to do."

Some of the passengers began to yell instructions.

"Turn the boat back!"

"Land'er anyway!"

"We'll be safer on Alcatraz!"

Nearly a full minute passed before the thunder stopped. We listened. A new sound was rising, a sound so terrible I choked back tears. It was a chorus of human cries.

At that, the captain shouted, "We're landing. Those who wish to remain aboard, may. All who want to disembark in San-Fran-cisco, I wish you God's speed."

I was overwhelmed by what was happening. Had I really seen buildings fall? What about our trip? Where was my bag? I wanted to shut my ears to those heartbreaking cries.

Mr. Irvine held Edith's shoulders. "Edie, I must get to City Hall immediately. If the trolleys aren't running, I'll walk there, by God. Who knows what hooligans are helping themselves to our documents. Now, if the captain cannot help you board the *Susanna,* then you must return to Stockton, is that clear? I will telephone Mother." He turned to leave.

Edith fingered her collar anxiously. Her eyes filled with tears at having to say good-bye to her father so suddenly. "What should we do, Daisy?"

"I . . . don't know. We're safe here at least, but maybe we should follow your father."

We felt a bump as the *Maria* hit a dock that slanted dangerously into the water. A man jumped off the bow with the line, then wrapped it around a cleat the size of a bed.

I could see the back of Mr. Irvine's head among the passengers swarming for the gangplank. Shouts pierced the air. Edith's eyes were wide with the same confusion I felt. A lantern swinging from a deck beam made her long hair look crimson. Suddenly I was shoved away from her.

"Edith!" I cried, trying to reach her outstretched arms. She disappeared from sight as the crowd crushed between us. I began to cry. As I felt myself being pressed forward, I saw our luggage. Quickly I bent to pick up the two smaller satchels, then with shuffling steps and my arms pinned to my sides, I let myself be pushed.

I couldn't see anything except a man's black coat in front of me and black sleeves to the right. Where was I going? Where was Edith?

The deck dropped off, and I would have fallen were it not for an unseen hand that held me. We were on the gangplank, going down toward the water. When my feet hit the dock the crowd opened up, and that's when I saw Edith off to the side, waving frantically and screaming my name. She managed to push her way to me and grab my elbow, her camera bag in her other hand.

"Daisy, I was so scared!" she shouted above the clamor. I answered by nodding and trying to dry my cheeks with my shoulder.

Some minutes later we saw Mr. Irvine standing on a wall, searching for us. Jumping down, he called, "I had a feeling you girls might be behind me, the way folks were shoving. We'll stay together. Come!" He took one of my bags—the one with our tickets, money, and maps. Our trunks remained on board.

We pressed along Drumm Street. Crowds of men and women with children, all in various states of undress, had begun fleeing from the city, apparently hoping to escape by boat. The shock of seeing these people, many weeping and some with bloodied clothes, made a part of me go numb.

I walked between Edith and Mr. Irvine. The ground jerked again, making me slip like I did my first time on ice skates. As they helped me up, I saw the tower of the ferry building several blocks away. The hands of the giant clock, two minutes fast, had stopped at 5:15.

It was April 18, 1906. Wednesday.

When I found myself in the street alone and under a
mass of clanging wires overhead I realized the danger was just as great,
as any minute I might be struck by a live wire if they came down, so I
ran almost another block away from flying brick, falling chimneys
and collapsing buildings to get into an open space.

Chapter 4

DUST FILLED THE AIR. Buildings gaped like doll-houses, their fronts peeled away. Iron beds, tables, hat racks, a commode, and wall paintings were in full view.

I was embarrassed to see several naked men run out of a hotel at the corner of Commercial Street.

From the rooms upstairs came the hysterical voices of women. One with peroxided hair waved a petticoat like a flag, screaming for help. The men disappeared into the crowded street.

"What can we do?" I asked Mr. Irvine.

He looked at the helpless woman, then he looked at me. "I don't know, honey. For now, let's keep going. The sooner we get to City Hall, the better. Edith, are you all right? Daisy? From the looks of things, we have quite a trek ahead of us. There'll be no trolleys today, I'm afraid."

It was difficult keeping pace with Mr. Irvine, even though he kept glancing back to make sure I was near. I worried he and Edith might get too far ahead and lose me. I'd never been to a city before. The fear of being lost among strangers made me walk faster.

Parts of the street were so full of stones and chunks of fallen chimneys that Edith and I had to hike up our skirts to step over the rubble. Several times, in my panic to keep up with her, I tripped.

Ahead, we saw four men clawing through bricks to uncover an unconscious woman. When she was free, one of the men scooped her into his arms. "Sarah!" he cried. Her nightdress was torn and her hair was covered with plaster. Near her was a little white bassinet. It was under part of a wall, crushed like an eggshell. My eyes filled with tears.

"Oh dear," said Edith. She set her bag down then took my hand. "This is dreadful. . . . This is terrible."

An angry shout drew our attention to a trolley car. It had been bounced onto its side like a broken toy. A photographer was on top, swinging his tripod at two policemen.

"You can't do that!" he yelled as another officer heaved a camera into the street, shattering it.

"That poor man," Edith said to me.

"What's happening?"

"Apparently they don't want him to take pictures."

"But why?"

Edith glanced over her shoulder. "I'm not sure. But I think we should be careful. . . . Where's Papa? Daisy, where'd he go?" She looked around, frantic. "Papa!"

"He can't be far," I said.

"Papa!" Edith ran through the crowd to the corner and looked each way, calling for him. There were many men in hats, walking, hurrying, shouting— but no sign of her father.

I rushed to her with the bags. When she threw her arms up in despair, I realized how Mr. Irvine had made me feel safe. Suddenly the idea of our travels no longer seemed fun. I did not feel brave, and I did not feel safe.

We continued in the direction of City Hall, uphill, alongside trolley tracks that were twisted like pipe cleaners. The harbor was at our back. Dozens upon dozens of people passed us on their way to the ferries. Edith craned her neck, trying to catch sight of her father. Often we were forced to turn sideways as we edged our way through the crowds, our bags bumping against legs and arms.

Families dragged their possessions on wagons, roller skates, sewing-machine tables—anything with wheels. Mothers pushed baby carriages loaded with bedding, a child or two riding on top, an infant on a hip. Rolled-up mattresses were carried on men's shoulders. Every minute or so young men rode by on bicycles.

Scattered among the debris were household items dropped by tired arms. Mine ached from carrying the bag. When I saw a pram tilted on a broken wheel I inspected it, relieved there wasn't an abandoned baby inside. A blue blanket trimmed in lace, a child's bonnet, and one white shoe were all.

"Edith," I called. I opened my satchel and understood why it was so heavy. It was filled with her glass plates.

"Oh, Daisy," she said, hurrying to my side. "What would I do without you? This will make walking so much easier. We might be able to reach Papa now."

I hid her two cameras, a small tarp, and the folding tripod under the blanket. Now policemen might think we were just two ladies with a baby. Most important, though, we could catch up to Mr. Irvine. It was still possible our ship would sail that afternoon, and he had our tickets.

*Quiver after quiver followed and now and then a heavier
shock, until it seemed as if the very heart of this old earth was broken
and was throbbing and dying away
slowly and gently.*

Chapter 5

WE STAYED IN THE MIDDLE of the street. Pushing
a pram with a crooked wheel was harder than I'd
thought it would be, made worse by so much rubble.
Often the crowd pressed between us and my heart
would race in panic until I was able to again catch
sight of Edith's long red hair. The thought of being

separated from her filled me with terror. Where would I go? What would I do?

San Francisco was a city Edith knew well. Her grandfather and great-uncles had ridden horseback here in the gold-rush days of saloons and miners' tents. She had told me about "gold fever" and how sailors had jumped ship in the bay, such was their hurry to reach land. The harbor had been so full of bare masts in those days, it had looked like a forest. Some of the empty boats were even hauled ashore to be used as hotels.

Now San Francisco was a city with mansions and streetcars. Edith and I struggled against the stream of refugees. The rumble of trunks being dragged along the street was as loud as thunder. Many ladies wore silk hats and jeweled brooches like the ones I'd seen on Mrs. Irvine. Two men with top hats and ivory-tipped canes sauntered along as if on their way to the opera.

"I can't believe it," Edith shouted above the noise. She swept her arm toward a row of wooden buildings that had splintered like toothpicks.

"Daisy, everything is in ruins. My cousins are here . . . friends. Tess Kern—you remember Tess, don't you, Dr. Willy's sister?—well, she lives on Union Street, and she has a new little baby. Aunt

Frances and Uncle Jim are at Folsom and Eleventh, in a beautiful house, just beautiful. Has it fallen like these?

"And Papa! How did we lose each other? What if City Hall is destroyed, too?"

I wanted to comfort Edith but did not know how. Except for becoming lost, my only worries were for my sorry old cat and my pa, who was mining at Carson Hill. Surely the earthquake hadn't reached there.

Edith's life was more complicated than mine. Her relatives owned ranches and businesses throughout California, San Francisco being the hub of their doings. Often she had described for me the elegant homes, the sophisticated commercial district, and the estates overlooking the bay. Her father's friends were na-bobs, some of the richest, most powerful men in the country.

Now I was trying to see the broken city through her eyes.

I felt for the pocket watch pinned to my blouse. The case clicked when I opened it. Though it was nearly seven o'clock in the morning, the sun was hidden by clouds of dust. Every few minutes, it seemed, the earth trembled, each time shaking loose more bricks and dust. As we walked, Edith searched the crowds for familiar faces, slowing sometimes to call a name. After an hour she stopped near a deserted alley.

"Well, Daisy, these aren't the streets of Paris, but there certainly is history staring at us. Think you're up to a little work?"

"Yes, ma'am!"

"I want to find Papa, but I also want to make use of our being here."

This was like her, to set aside her worries—temporarily—while she did what she needed to do. Right now she was a photographer, recording history as it unfolded.

I looked for policemen. I hoped I would spot Mr. Irvine instead.

She leaned into the buggy. Her hands were under the blanket, sliding one of the glass plates into her camera. Meanwhile, I pulled out her tripod, expanded the legs, then locked them in place by tightening the brass butterfly screws. Edith lifted her camera to the tiny square platform. To me it looked like a bread box. How it would transform these people into a shiny photograph mystified me.

A man watched Edith with curiosity, then went on his way. I unfolded the little tarp so she could spread it over the camera, then duck underneath. After a few moments I heard the shutter click. I handed her the wooden case so she could slip the plate in without exposing it to light. We repeated this four times; and each time, growing more nervous by the minute, I made sure we were not being observed. When she was finished, I rolled up the tarp and helped her undo the tripod.

The instant she hid her camera a vibration started beneath our feet, low at first, then as loud as if the locomotive had returned. Edith and I were thrown down as the ground rolled under us, popping up cobblestones. The buildings seemed to grind against each other. Dust exploded upward. Voices shrieked.

A milkman whipped his rearing horse, trying to steer it away from a collapsing wall. The horse screamed in fright but managed to pull ahead just in time. Everything seemed to be happening in slow motion.

I watched a chimney sway back and forth, then snap. It crashed, scattering so close to us that a brick struck my arm. Blood began to spread through the white of my sleeve. I stared as if it were someone else's arm. The pain seemed distant.

"Whenever will this stop? . . . Are you all right,

Daisy?" Edith was struggling to her feet. She pulled out her handkerchief. Her blue eyes showed concern as she bent to bandage my cut.

"There you are," she said, pulling me up. "Does it hurt much?"

"A little."

We brushed off our skirts. It was a strange thought, but I wondered if my hair was messy. My scalp ached from the pins and from not being brushed last night. Was that why Edith refused to wear her hair up?

"Someone, please!" came a cry, distracting me. In front of a corner grocery store was a large woman wearing a nightdress and garden boots. She waved her arm frantically. In her other arm was a plump, rosy-cheeked baby. Green-and-white-striped awnings hung in tatters over windows that, oddly enough, were not broken.

When the woman saw us approach she called to someone inside.

"Thank the Lord you're here," she said to us. "Poor Mr. Somers is stuck!"

I rested the buggy on its broken wheel so it wouldn't roll away. We found the store in chaos. Floor-to-ceiling shelves were empty, their contents scattered on the floor. In the center of a narrow

aisle sat a man buried up to his neck in an assortment of dried beans. I knew it wasn't polite to laugh,
but I did, a loud "Haw!" A man stuck in a pile of
beans was the funniest thing I'd ever seen. Quickly
I covered my mouth, pretending to cough. A lady
Edith's age was already trying to dig him out. We
kneeled next to her and began scooping beans away.

"It was that last shock that did it," Mrs. Somers
said. "Eight-fourteen sharp, and everything that didn't
fall the first time fell then. Mercy!"

When Mr. Somers's arms were free we hoisted
him up. I say "hoist" because he was as big as a
horse. His apron was smeared with tomatoes and
broken eggs, but he was as cheerful as someone who's
just eaten lunch.

"Ladies, I thank you. Are you all right, dear?" he
asked his wife.

"I have never seen such a mess in my life, Harold. Yes, baby Timothy and I are fine," she said.

The younger woman, pretty and plump as a hen,
turned to us. "My name is Mary Exa," she said with
a southern drawl. "I live upstairs. Mr. and Mrs. Somers
are my landlords and this, I am afraid, is what remains of their lovely store."

Edith introduced herself, then took my hand. "This
is my assistant, Daisy Valentine. We were to set sail

for Australia this afternoon, but I suspect tonight we'll be going up the river instead, back to Stockton—but on which boat, I don't know. Our trunks are probably lost now and all our tickets. The docks are such a mess I doubt any ships will be able—"

"Oh, but your father," I interrupted, "he has our tickets and money. There's still time to find him, and then there are still several hours before the *Susanna* leaves."

"How unusual," Mrs. Somers replied after thinking a moment. "You both are so young to travel alone, but it sounds like a wonderful enterprise. I heartily approve. Your plans have been spoiled, though; how dreadful for you girls. . . . Mercy, where are my manners? You must be famished. Mr. Somers, let's see what we can offer our rescuers, shall we?" She chattered happily, as if earthquakes were an everyday adventure. Weren't the Somerses aware of the devastation beyond their store?

Edith exchanged stories with the others, asking opinions, listening. She seemed lighthearted, but when she mentioned her father, she burst into tears. I started to cry, too, seeing her distress.

While our new friends consoled us, I counted my sorrows: the idea of returning to Moke Hill so soon filled me with despair. All those months of dreaming and enduring! For an instant I felt desperate enough to run back to the harbor, even to abandon Edith—anything to avoid living again under Mrs. Irvine's iron will.

Why hadn't I let Mr. Irvine carry the other bag so that I'd now have the one with the tickets? Edith had family, position, and enough wealth to plan another trip anytime she wanted. If we didn't find Mr. Irvine, her dream would be merely postponed. Mine would be lost.

*There was over $500 worth of bottle goods broken
in their store—piled knee deep behind the counters where it fell from the
shelves. Such a mess of broken glass, jellies, jams, pickles,
fruit, wines, whiskies, etc., smeared
and flowing around.*

Chapter 6

MR. AND MRS. SOMERS were gracious hosts. From
the rubble of their store they salvaged canned peaches
and tins of Scottish shortbread. Mary Exa, however,
returned from the backyard pump with her pitcher
empty.

"There is no water," she said slowly. "Not a drop."

We all looked at her. I was thirsty. I knew Edith must be, too. Why hadn't we thought to travel with canteens?

Mrs. Somers handed me her wiggly baby. His diaper felt like a soggy dishcloth as he settled into my arms. I wanted to hand him back, but he gave me such a sweet smile that I didn't. I tried not to think about the crushed bassinet we'd seen earlier.

Meanwhile Mrs. Somers had waded through the aisle of beans to an oak icebox in the corner. She unlatched a bottom door. Below the melting chunk of ice was a pan. She tipped it into the pitcher and returned, proudly, with enough water for us to sip, twice around.

After Mrs. Somers put some shortbread into our pram, she opened her arms for her baby. I was happy to return him. An unpleasant odor made me sniff my wet sleeves, but the smell was not from Timothy.

Something was burning.

Mr. Somers pointed toward the harbor. Several plumes of black smoke rose in the sky.

"Dear me, I believe the market district's on fire," said Mary Exa.

Mr. Somers was still pointing. ". . . nine . . .

ten . . . eleven. . . . Eleven separate fires. Chief Sullivan is going to be busy this morning, yes sirree."

"Chief Sullivan," Mary Exa explained to us in her drawl, "has an outstanding department, the best in California. San Francisco is safe in his hands." Mary Exa, too, was in her nightdress, with a smock buttoned over it. It was an odd outfit, but I supposed she'd been interrupted getting ready for work. Her brown hair was neatly coiled on top of her head, as if she had just spent time in front of a mirror. She wore a hat, and her round face dimpled when she smiled.

Mr. Somers disappeared into the store for a few minutes. When he returned he had three chairs and one stool.

"Ladies," he said after arranging the chairs on the sidewalk, "Chief Sullivan is one of our regular customers, and he knows how this neighborhood loves to watch a fire. Have a seat." He bowed as far as his large stomach would allow.

Mrs. Somers sat down. Timothy nuzzled her shirt until he found an opening between the buttons, then began nursing contentedly. Edith and I sat, too. It felt good to rest my feet, and it felt good to be with folks who cared about us. Suddenly I realized how tired I was, and how hungry. I wanted to search for Mr. Irvine, but I also wanted to stay in this chair as if it were an ordinary afternoon on the Irvines' porch.

"Yes," Mrs. Somers continued. "Mrs. Sullivan prefers our walnuts and avocados to the ones at Bettini's Market around the corner, but don't get me wrong, the Bettinis are fine folks. You can't find a better salami than at Bettini's. Hello, Mr. and Mrs. Westlake!"

An elderly couple, white-haired and hatless, was hurrying by, carrying a bird cage between them. Inside the cage was a terrified cat, meowing loudly.

"Daisy and Edith, these here are our neighbors," said Mrs. Somers. She made introductions from her seat.

The Westlakes stopped, relieved to accept the bench offered by Mr. Somers. They told how their canaries flew away when the cage fell over, then how they rescued their cat seconds before a chimney crashed onto their bed. Mrs. Westlake was breathless from the retelling.

"I hollered to the Davenports, but they didn't answer. Not a word. I'm afraid something horrible has happened," she said. At this Mrs. Westlake broke out sobbing. "It's worse than the ones in 'sixty-five and 'sixty-eight. Now there are fires *everywhere.*"

"Don't worry, Chief Sullivan is on his way." Mr. Somers spoke in a consoling tone, as if the chief himself had just delivered this news.

We turned to the sound of horses galloping toward us. There were four of them, all white, loosely hitched together, their reins flapping to the sides. Behind them bounced the bright red tongue of a wagon.

"There's supposed to be a steamer with them horses," said Mr. Westlake. "Why, they're from Station Eleven up there on Front Street, I believe."

He turned to Mr. Somers. "How in the name of John Henry is the chief going to get to those fires if his horses aren't connected to the engine? You tell me."

Without warning, there was another jolt. Mrs. Somers dashed into the middle of the street with baby Timothy, followed by Mary Exa; Mrs. Westlake ran, too, dragging her bird cage. The men had fallen off their chairs. Edith and I clung to each other, watching nervously as electric wires swung overhead. Several fell nearby with a popping sound, blue smoke hissing from their torn ends.

The horses passed us and continued in a panic down the street, as if chased by an imaginary demon. Their muscular flanks and a wild tangle of their manes was all I saw as a wall swayed out over the street and collapsed on top of them.

We stared in stunned silence. Within a tumble of bricks lay the four horses, white and still as marble. The only sound was the trickling of dirt. I caught my breath at the horror of it, the suddenness.

"It happened so fast. . . . If only we could have stopped them," Edith said, her eyes filling with tears.

After several moments, she considered the buggy. "I don't want them to be forgotten," she said softly, pulling out one of her cameras. I looked around and, not seeing any policemen, unfolded the tripod and tarp. With her foot she began clearing stones away, making a space wide enough to plant her tripod.

I was beginning to understand what photography meant to Edith. It was her way of saving things. It was a way to push aside her sorrow.

"They were magnificent, weren't they, Daisy?"

I went up to the Somers then and they had the nerve to be cooking breakfast, not knowing how bad things were. It was a miracle that they were not blown up . . . as the gas pipes were all broken and many explosions occurred that way.

Chapter 7

WE HID THE EXPOSED plates under the buggy's thin mattress. Edith used three more plates to photograph upturned trolley tracks and the broken houses along Mary Exa's street. She carefully covered everything with the blue, lace-edged blanket.

Edith, Mary Exa, and I spoke little as we wandered around the neighborhood, not in a hurry to return to Somers's Grocery. Everywhere we looked people crowded the streets, some hauling baggage and children to the ferries. Others, like us, milled around, unsure what to do. Edith looked twice at anyone resembling her father.

"Daisy," she said after a while, "we're still a distance from City Hall. There's a chance Papa has found his way there already and is waiting for us, but it could take us hours. See."

Edith pointed to the harbor where plumes of smoke grew taller and darker by the second. The fire was spreading. Was City Hall in danger? I opened my watch. It was still early, ten minutes after nine.

Dust prevented the sun from casting even the grayest of shadows. My mouth was dry. I was thirsty again and even hungrier than before. If we did try to reach City Hall, how long would it take us, and when we got there, would we be able to find Mr. Irvine? There were so many people everywhere. Then, if we did find him and were able to get our tickets, would we make it back to the harbor in time to board the *Susanna*?

Up ahead some men were dipping paintbrushes into a can and writing on a long plank of wood. They nailed it between two telegraph poles in front of Alta Drug Store. The white letters read:

SEWERS BLOCKED. DON'T USE TOILETS.
EPIDEMIC THREATENED.
OBEY ORDERS OR GET SHOT.

I had heard that in big cities some homes and hotels had indoor toilets instead of privies. This message upset me.

"Do you think they're serious?" I asked. "They'll shoot us?"

"Nonsense." Edith laughed. "There's not a man alive who would shoot a lady for doing what she needs to do."

A gunshot from the warehouse area silenced us. We looked at one another. The sign seemed more serious now.

"We'll be safe with Mr. and Mrs. Somers," said Mary Exa. "There is privacy in their backyard. Some shrubs, a tree. We'll just . . ." Mary Exa began to blush, then she turned away as if speaking to someone else. "We'll just . . . dig a hole. Won't we?"

We entered the cluttered market and parked the pram inside the doorway. The delicious aroma of frying ham greeted us. Mary Exa rushed upstairs.

"Mrs. Somers!" she yelled, taking two steps at a time. "Mrs. Somers, put out your fire!"

There was a clamor overhead, voices, some stomping. Edith and I hurried out back to a yard barely large enough to hold a wagon. I lifted the pump handle, then dropped it. It made a hollow clank.

"We're in some pickle now, aren't we, Daisy? No water, we've lost Papa, and it may be impossible to catch a boat back to Stockton tonight. I wonder if Mother has any idea of what's happened. . . . Oh, how I'd love to wash my face."

"Me, too," I said. "I would sell my shoes for a drink." For the moment, I was too tired to tell her that the boat we should think about catching was the one sailing for Australia.

Edith leaned against the fence. Her sleeves were rolled up and she combed her fingers through her long hair. We were both as dusty as ranch hands. We listened to the noise of the Somerses and West- lakes clomping down the stairs. The men appeared in the yard with blankets and two mattresses. Mrs. Somers carried baby Timothy in one arm, a frying pan of ham in the other. Mrs. Westlake's cat was still yowling from inside the cage. Mary Exa had grabbed an assortment of clothes.

"Ladies," she said to Edith and me, "please take no offense when I offer you a fresh change. There is a blouse for each of you, and two petticoats. Unfortunately, there is only one spare hat, but I do have a hairbrush I'm more than happy to give you."

Mary Exa leaned close to whisper. "It's a shame I'm unable to offer you genuine southern hospitality, in particular a nice hot bath and a—"

She was interrupted by a powerful jolt. I screamed. We all fell to the grass.

"Lord, have mercy!" yelled Mrs. Somers. The fence shook as if children were climbing it. The sounds of glass breaking and bricks falling from the chimney were frightening. More dust filled the air.

In a moment it was quiet. Edith and I exchanged looks of relief, touching each other for reassurance as we stood. We draped a blanket over a bush in the corner of the yard and extended it with a rake handle, then took turns changing into fresh blouses. We brushed out our hair. The cut on my arm was sore but no longer bleeding. I helped Mary Exa button into a blue dress with a high collar. She looked quite elegant.

Edith fastened her new waistcoat, then picked up the hat. After considering it thoughtfully, she handed it to me.

"Here you go, Daisy," she said. "It seems silly to think about our wardrobes at a time like this, but I do feel better somehow." The hat was a smooth velvet, midnight blue with a pink rose at the crown. It was beautiful.

Too pleased to say anything, I just put it on, tilting it to the side like Mary Exa's. If only Pa could see me now. My hair was up and I wore a clean white blouse with puffed sleeves, and now, a hat. I felt so good, I laughed out loud. Now the disappointments of the day didn't make me ache quite so much.

*The big fire in the mission [district] was caused by
a man and woman who, after being made to put out the first fire they
made, built another as soon as the policeman left. He came back,
saw what they had done, called them out
and shot them dead.*

Chapter 8

IT WAS ALMOST ELEVEN o'clock in the morning.
A powerful hunger gnawed in me, made worse by
my thirst. The ground seemed to quiver every few
minutes, like a train shuddering to a stop. It made
us afraid to enter the building, because with every
shake something new would fall.

Mr. Somers had taken off his apron and was now dressed in a vest, a tweed cap, and a coat, for the day was cool. He and the elderly Mr. Westlake made several trips into the market to retrieve groceries that had not burst open or been pebbled with broken glass.

When they brought out a basket of oranges, my mouth began to water. I bit into one, not even bothering to peel it, and began sucking the sweet juice. We fell hungrily on soda crackers with pink frosting, then on walnuts, which we shelled by smacking them with a stone.

Suddenly Edith stood, brushing her skirt. "Daisy, I've got to get to City Hall somehow. If you're not too tired could you come with me?"

"Of course."

"Edith, are you leaving?" asked Mary Exa. She handed a sleeping Timothy back to his mother. He was freshly diapered in remnants from my blouse.

"I can't rest until I find my father." Edith opened the broken gate for us, then went to the front of the store for the baby carriage.

A soldier was hammering a notice onto a telephone pole. He shouldered his rifle, then winked. I didn't like the slippery way he looked at us.

When he had gone we read the sign.

"This is illegal," Edith said. "It's not constitutional."

"What is it? What's happened?" asked Mr. Somers. He read aloud:

PROCLAMATION BY THE MAYOR

The Federal Troops, the members of the Regular Police Force, and all the Special Police Officers have been authorized to *KILL* any and all persons found engaged in Looting or in the Commission of Any Other Crime.

I have directed all the Gas and Electric Lighting Co.'s not to turn on Gas or Electricity until I order them to do so. You may therefore expect the city to remain in darkness for an indefinite time.

I request all citizens to remain at home from darkness until daylight every night until order is restored.

I WARN all Citizens of the danger of fire from Damaged or Destroyed Chimneys, Broken or Leaking Gas Pipes or Fixtures, or any like cause.

E. E. Schmitz, Mayor

"Fancy that scoundrel!" Mr. Somers said, turning to us. "Next thing you know, he'll have families shot for cooking supper." He laughed so hard he began to cough. When he saw my confused look, he took off his cap and held it in front of him.

"Forgive me, ladies. You being visitors to our city probably don't know Mayor Schmitz is one of the biggest looters there is. Him and his crony Abe Reuf have been stealing folks blind, turning public property into private places for them and their slimy pals. Mr. Westlake," he called over the fence, "take a look at this!

"It's no secret the mayor's been up to no good for a long time," Mr. Somers said to me. "Why, rumor has it he could be sent to San Quentin on account of graft and bribery. But no telling what'll happen now, what with this earthquake an' all. Maybe God has His own way of shaking things up." He laughed again.

Mr. Westlake joined us on the corner. His beard was long and white, making me think of kindly old Saint Nick. After reading the poster, he chuckled. Hands in pockets, he rocked on his heels.

"Well, well. First the fox raids the henhouse, then he tells the farmer to shoot the ones that get away. There's nothin' new under the sun, is there, Harold?" Mr. Westlake smiled at his friend.

"No sir, that's the God's truth," said Mr. Somers.

*Out came a little man with bloody feet who
had escaped a big falling mirror, clad in the thinnest little tights.*

Chapter 9

MARY EXA INSISTED on going with us to City Hall.
We followed the parade of oddly dressed people.
Those trying to escape to Oakland were crowded
along North Street in front of the ferry building. An
assortment of ferries, tugs, and fishing trawlers were
chugging across the wide, cold bay. Whistles shrieked
from the little boats as if encouraging one another.

I could not see the *Maria* or a ship that might be the *Susanna*.

There were so many fires now that the smoke was rising to form one black, billowing cloud. We headed up Market Street away from the harbor and blended into the confusion. Once again I became uneasy, trying not to lose sight of Edith. It was impossible to keep people from crowding between us.

The noise was great. Men shouted to each other as they cleared a path wide enough for horses to pull the steam engines through. Each engine that rushed by was armed with a large brass bell that clanged wildly. Ambulance wagons were also urgent with bells.

Because there was so much commotion and no policemen were in sight, Edith decided it was safe to take pictures. Though desperate to find her father, she was still a practical artist, making use of every moment. It was peculiar we'd seen almost no one else with cameras.

Everywhere we looked people dug desperately at bricks and boards. Edith often slowed down to gaze at a storefront or a group of people. She studied each scene before setting up her equipment.

We developed a swift routine as photographer and assistant. Mary Exa was our nervous lookout.

Several times she spotted soldiers eyeing us, so we quickly hovered over the carriage as if we were doting aunties, the photo abandoned. We didn't really know why we needed to hide. We just knew, for now at least, that we had to.

One of the grandest buildings I'd ever seen was up ahead. It was eight stories high and filled one square block. An American flag flew from a pole on the roof.

"All the nabobs stay here," explained Mary Exa. "Rich people, mining kings, actors, that sort. Why, the first thing I did when I arrived from Louisiana was to have lunch in their lovely tearoom. The Palace Hotel is made with so much stone, ladies, it'll never burn. We're safe here."

When I looked at the sky, I wasn't sure. It was darker than thunderclouds ready to burst. The smells of burning wood and something bitter like paint or rubber were strong. It seemed odd that the fire was so close and folks weren't clearing out.

Suddenly, the driver of an engine pulled his horses to a stop and the crew jumped down. One man put a wrench to the hydrant while two others twisted a hose onto the tank. With a rallying cry, another ran to the end of the hose and lifted the shiny brass nozzle. Seconds passed. The man with the wrench threw his weight into opening the valve. Finally he dropped his hands.

"She's empty here, too, lads. God help us!"

The firefighters raced to another hydrant half a block away. A man in an evening cloak and top hat helped lead the horses. A boy followed, dragging the flat beige hoses. He was thin and eager, with a hat pulled over his ears.

More yells announced there was no water anywhere in sight. A narrow building taller than the Palace Hotel was surrounded by smaller stores that were smoking from the heat. I could hear crackling, like wood breaking apart.

"That's the *Call* building," said Mary Exa, pointing up the street. "One of our newspapers is printed there. Claus Spreckels built it with his sugar money. Oh, I can't believe it might burn, too. I have a gentleman friend—he's an editor there—and now, quite frankly, I am worried for his safety." Mary Exa spoke as rapidly as her drawl would allow.

I was distracted by a squat man in a fur coat shrieking in a foreign language. A white towel was wrapped around his neck. Under one arm he carried a portrait of our president, Theodore Roosevelt. He gestured angrily with his other hand. Finally, he yelled in English.

"I never come back here! Never to Sanna Francisco again! Never!" He stalked toward the hotel lobby and began to yell at a Chinese man who was pushing a trunk outside.

"Why, I do believe I saw that man last night," Mary Exa said. "At the opera. Mrs. Somers and I went to see *Carmen,* and he was a magnificent Don Jose."

"Who is he?" I asked.

Mary Exa pulled her shoulders erect. "Enrico Caruso, the most famous tenor in the world, from Italy. He's on a world tour with the New York Metropolitan Opera. Daisy, if you could hear him. Such a voice."

"I do hear him," I said.

She and Edith laughed. I liked that, their laugh. Mary Exa's hat hid part of her face, emphasizing her graceful neck. Her full figure was enhanced by the cut of her dress and the bell sleeves buttoning at her wrists. I don't think she had spent one day in the sun, as her skin was creamy white. I could picture her watching the Great Caruso onstage.

I could picture Edith there, too. She was slightly taller and thinner than Mary Exa, with the same dignified bearing. Her hair falling loose down her back made her look different from most women her age but not in a bad way. Edith had the ruddy, freckled complexion of redheads who do not shade their faces outdoors. She didn't seem to be troubled that she was one of the few ladies who did not wear hats or pin their hair up.

It was this renegade side of Edith that Dr. Willy adored. This he had happily confessed to me last Christmas after she bumped into him under the mistletoe. I must admit, I enjoyed this side of Edith, too.

What I did not enjoy, however, was that she and Mary Exa were chatting as if we were on a picnic.

The longer it took us to reach City Hall, the less likely it was that we'd find Mr. Irvine or that he'd find us. And we had to find him if we were ever to sail for Australia.

The sidewalks were covered with fallen chimneys and broken window glass, and it was dangerous to walk near the houses on account of hanging stone, bricks, etc., which would come down with every little quake.

Chapter 10

I WAS TRYING TO LIFT the baby carriage over a chunk of cement when a man staggered into me. He wore a tuxedo and silk top hat.

" 'Scuse me, miss. I was juss bringin' this to a lady fren." His words were slurred, and when he held up two brandy glasses—one near empty—I understood why.

"Mr. Barrymore!" someone called to him. "Over here! Madame Reesa is over here."

Mr. Barrymore raised both glasses. "Cheers!" he said before sloshing back the tallest drink.

I backed away from him. He was dapper and handsome as they come, but I knew the smell of a drunk. Edith leaned forward to get a good look at his face.

"Are you *John* Barrymore?" she asked. "The actor?"

"I am, I am, I am! Yes, ma'am, I am! And I found madame a drink at the Bohemian Club. We've had such a terrible thirst." Mr. Barrymore paused to swallow, which brought forth an enormous hiccup.

He began weaving toward a lady sitting on a trunk near the entrance. She wore a feathered cape and matching hat. Her legs were crossed in such a way that her skirt pulled up, revealing high-heeled shoes buttoned below the ankle. I may have been raised in a mining camp, but I knew one thing for sure: a lady does not show her ankles unless it's an emergency. Pa taught me that much.

"How do you know John Barrymore?" Mary Exa asked Edith.

"I like to read theater notices and reviews of books in *Current Literature,* sometimes the *Overland.* I saw he was playing the lead in Richard Harding Davis's new play."

"Yes, *The Dictator.*" Mary Exa fanned her face and laughed as she said this. "He was dreadful. We saw him last Saturday evening. Pity. His company is supposed to sail this afternoon for Australia, but it doesn't look like he'll make it, poor fellow."

"Did you say *Australia?*" Edith asked. "That's right! We were to see his play in Melbourne. I wonder what ship he was booked on."

"Oh, I wouldn't know."

"Daisy, do you suppose . . ."

I didn't wait for Edith to finish. "Mr. Barrymore," I called, hurrying toward him. "What was the name of your ship?"

He cleared his throat and, with his fingers delicately against his throat, began to sing. "Oh, Susanna! Oh, don't shoo cry for me. . . ."

"The *Susanna?* Sir, could you tell me . . . do you know . . . is she still sailing this afternoon? She's our ship, too. Edith . . . I knew it! It's not too late. We can still go."

He sat on the trunk with the lady. Looking bored, he leisurely crossed his legs, then lit a cigarette. Holding it dramatically to the side, he gazed skyward.

"Sunk like a stone. Captain kilt, too."

"She sank?"

"Dreadful, *n'est-ce pas?*" He giggled.

"But that's not fair," I cried.

Mr. Barrymore shrugged, then turned back to his companion. Edith gently led me away. "It's not fair," I sobbed.

"Oh, Daisy," she said. "I'm disappointed, too."

It seemed we were going in circles rather than straight to City Hall. There was so much debris blocking streets and alleys, we were constantly retracing our steps. Every time the crowd flowed between us, I felt increasingly frantic. My throat ached from crying.

Finally we maneuvered around some uneven piles of brick off Sansome Street and stopped. Down the block a scramble of men was bending, gathering, hurrying. Cautiously Edith reached into the buggy for her telephoto camera.

"Looters?" I asked. She nodded.

"Look at all those shoes," Mary Exa whispered.

Even though we were partly hidden by an overturned wagon, I felt nervous that Edith wanted to photograph looters. Mary Exa kept looking behind and around us.

"Please," she said. "Maybe we should go, Edith."

"Yes, what if they see us? Please, Edith." I was afraid.

"We'll be quick. . . . Ready, Daisy?"

We crouched among broken boards. I opened the tripod but only extended the legs partway. Edith fastened the camera onto it, covered it with the tarp, then began studying the scene through her lens. I handed her a case with one of her largest glass plates.

"An eight-by-ten should show them all. . . . Wait. . . . I don't believe it. Daisy, look through here."

Edith leaned back so I could put my eye to the viewfinder. Immediately the men looked so close I could see the dark stripes down the sides of their trousers. The crowns of their hats were angular and there was writing on them. I squinted to read the words.

"U-nited . . . States . . ."

"What?" said Mary Exa. "Let me see, Daisy."

After a moment she looked at us and shook her head in disbelief.

"They're soldiers from our very own Fort Mason. Raiding a shoe store!"

Edith looked through the lens again, then released the shutter. Just as it clicked, we heard heavy footsteps in the gravel behind us.

"Such pretty things to be all alone," said a man's voice.

We froze.

Slowly the man walked around the wagon to face us. It was one of the soldiers. His rifle had a bayonet on the tip.

"Taking little pictures are you, miss?" He chuckled as he examined each of us head to toe. "Now why would you want to do a thing like that?"

Edith casually unbolted the camera from the tripod, then slid the plate into its sleeve. Though she seemed to ignore the soldier, I could see that the color had drained from her face.

"Here, Daisy." She handed me the camera. It was the heavy one of cherry wood with brass trim. I was so nervous my arms were shaking. Just as I put it into the buggy, the soldier grabbed the plate from Edith.

"I asked you a question, little Miss Fo-tog-raf-fer!" He pulled the plate out of its case, then flung it to the middle of the street, where it burst with a tinkling sound.

I could hear Mary Exa catch her breath, but Edith

didn't flinch. Her eyes narrowed. I knew she was mad.

The soldier aimed his gun. First at Mary Exa, whose chin was quivering. He pointed at me, then Edith. He stepped forward until the bayonet touched Edith's shoulder.

I started breathing more heavily. My heart raced. What could I do to help her? Mary Exa's dress rustled as she grabbed my arm. Should we run?

The soldier traced the blade along Edith's neck, then held it to her throat. Finally, he lowered the gun. His face was inches from hers.

With his hand he stroked her hair, then her shoulder. When he moved toward the front of her blouse, I saw a flash of Edith's skirt as she launched her knee between his legs.

His shout of surprise turned into a groan as he doubled over. The gun clattered to the ground. He tried to grab Edith's ankle, but she kicked his wrist.

"You . . . *little* . . ." was all he was able to say before I swung the tripod into his side. He rolled into a ball.

We ran. At the corner I realized I'd left the cameras behind.

"Daisy, no!" screamed Edith when I turned back.

The soldier was crawling on his elbows, trying to

reach his gun. He saw me. The instant he lunged for my skirt, I kicked gravel in his face. He roared an obscenity and blindly swatted the air. I heaved his rifle as far away as possible and began to drag the carriage behind me at an awkward run.

When I reached Edith, she pulled me to her with a sob.

*One woman was shot after being twice ordered to put out
a light and a man was hung and a sign placed on his body, saying "This
man was hung for stealing."*

Chapter 11

HALF AN HOUR LATER, Edith, still badly shaken, threw her hands up in frustration. Tears edged her voice. "I don't believe it. There's the Somerses' grocery store and we are . . . right . . . back where we started."

Confused, Mary Exa looked behind us, then up the hill. "I do apologize," she said. "All the years

I've lived here, and I, of all people, have been leading us in circles. Everything is such a mess! Edith,
we could at least take a rest since we're here. I
know *I* need to sit, and by the look of your face, so
do you."

We saw Mr. and Mrs. Somers as we trudged
uphill. They sat in chairs in front of their ruined
store with the Westlakes and another family. Three
red-haired little boys were stacking pieces of brick
into a miniature castle.

I rushed into Mrs. Somers's warm arms and let
her hold me. Her tender welcome made me want to
tell about the soldier, but there was such a flurry of
introductions that I didn't have a chance.

Mr. McGregor was the baker of the delicious
shortbread we'd eaten earlier. His wife, Molly, smiled
as if we were old friends. I liked her instantly. She
spoke in a pleasant Scottish brogue. The way her
wool smock draped off her shoulders, I knew she
was expecting a baby any day now.

Mrs. Westlake held my chin. "We started prayin',
Daisy, when we heard gunshots. Me and Mrs. Somers
were worried sick about you girls. I'm s'glad you
came back."

"Yes indeed, we worried," said Mr. Somers. "Especially on account of the fires. Our beautiful city is

burning by the mile. Every pipe in every block is busted; hydrants are empty. Some folks are desperate enough to use sewer water. Sewer water! Imagine."

Water. How I needed a drink! And there was so much dust on my hands and face I would have done almost anything to have a small bowl for washing.

As night began to fall an eerie glow emerged. The sky was red from the fire, which was growing by the second. We seemed safe enough at Somers's Grocery. For now, at least, I could rest my eyes and not worry about losing Edith.

Every few minutes a group of soldiers would pass by, some on horseback. I could not look at them. Edith and Mary Exa, obviously upset, whispered with Molly McGregor. Were they telling her about our soldier? I wanted to be included in their woman talk, so I left Mrs. Somers and hesitantly moved toward them.

A mattress had been spread for the children, but they were wound up tighter than alarm clocks and would not sleep. Molly was too uncomfortable to lie down, so we began making her a couch against the fence.

"Bless you, lassies," she said, out of breath. "Me home is gone . . . all me things . . . instead I hoff new friends, you. I'm better off, ye know." Molly smiled wearily but with tenderness. I envied the easy way she, Edith, and Mary Exa talked, as if they were sisters or longtime friends. Even though I was the youngest, I wanted to be her friend, too.

I sat on the ground and watched in silence as bugs filed from the broken wall of the house. They marched, unafraid, toward us. As they approached I realized they were cockroaches, huge brown ones the size of my thumb. I jumped onto a trunk and huddled there while the others stomped and swatted, trying to rid the yard of the horrible creatures.

After clearing the area and exhausting all our energy, we settled among the blankets and lumps of furniture. Oranges were shared, plus a jar of olives that had survived, tins of sardines, shortbread. Mr. Somers found a barrel of lemon drops. Into each of our pockets he put generous mounds of the sour candies.

"Children, when you're thirsty, pop one into your mouth like so." He made his lips form an O, then with his hand he clapped a candy into his mouth with a loud *pop!,* much to the boys' delight. Soon there was a game, and thirst was temporarily forgotten.

Unable to wash Timothy's diapers, we buried the

soiled ones and hung the wet ones over the fence to dry. The youngest McGregor boys needed a change of pants, too. From among the pile of clothes we found some sweaters. We slipped their little legs into the armholes and buttoned each sweater, then tied it at the boys' waists with shoelaces. They were now dry and warm as could be.

We sat together in the damp air, unable to sleep. I wrapped the hem of my skirt tightly around my ankles in case any cockroaches came near. The slightest movement made me jump, as if it were the beginning of another earthquake. I once cried out in fear, but the vibration was only the children tumbling in the grass like puppies.

"If the fire comes any nearer, we'll hoff to run for it," said Mr. McGregor. "Cun the missus and I count on ye to help us with the wee bairns?"

Yes, of course, we all said. I looked at Molly McGregor. Where was a lady supposed to go to have a baby, and how on earth would she get there if she was so miserable walking?

Molly was eating an orange Mrs. Somers had peeled for her. I never saw anyone enjoy an orange so much. Mrs. Westlake took over with Molly's little boys as if she had been their grandmother all along.

Including baby Timothy, there were thirteen of us that Wednesday night.

By five o'clock the next morning we had counted twenty-four jolts strong enough to knock a person down. Now it was Thursday. I had not slept since the boat.

Two policemen stood in the street, calling the residents out of their yards. We gathered around.

"You must leave immediately! Mayor Schmitz has ordered dynamiting this side of Van Ness to begin in half an hour!"

"Why, why?" were the cries.

"What ain't standing, ain't gonna burn. Sorry, folks, but you'll have to leave. Golden Gate Park is the nearest place to go."

Edith's face dropped. "How will we ever get to City Hall if streets are being dynamited? I knew we should have tried to get through last night, but I was just so exhausted. Do your blisters hurt as much as mine, Daisy?"

Yes, I nodded. But right now getting to City Hall was not my biggest worry. How would Molly McGregor make it to Golden Gate Park?

As I looked around us, I noticed something tucked in the alley under a broken tree.

"Edith, look—for Molly!" I pulled her sleeve until she followed me. When she saw the abandoned popcorn wagon, brightly painted red, with yellow wheels, she smiled at me.

"It's perfect, Daisy."

*Mr. Somers dug a great hole in the backyard and we buried
everything we could, even took up her [Mrs. Somers's] good carpet and
linoleum and put them in, they had a fine supply of
groceries which we buried.*

Chapter 12

THERE WERE WINDOWS up the four sides of the
popcorn wagon, all broken. We brushed the glass
out with a branch, lifted the wooden tongue between us, and hauled it to the corner.

Mr. McGregor and Mr. Somers were bravely
making dashes into the house. They gathered some
of Mrs. Somers's cherished items: her wedding dress,

a coffee grinder, and Timothy's baby cradle. These things and some food were buried in a large hole they dug in the yard.

The Westlakes tried to rescue belongings from their home but were turned away by soldiers.

We helped Molly McGregor up into the wagon. For a moment she clutched a rail and held her breath. Oblivious to her pain, her little sons clambered aboard, excited about the ride and hoping to find some popcorn. Timothy was propped up in a crate so he could look around.

Finally we were ready. With a great heave-ho, Mr. Somers and Mr. McGregor began pulling while the rest of us walked alongside and behind. We were as noisy as a caravan of gypsies.

Mrs. Westlake and Mrs. Somers looked back at their homes, at their neighborhood, their arms tight around each other. Tears streamed down their faces.

"Forty-three years," sobbed Mrs. Westlake. "They're going to blow up forty-three years. . . . My babies were born here. . . . My wedding quilt . . . my mother's necklace. . . . I didn't even say goodbye to the Davenports." At the mention of her friends' name she wailed at the burning sky.

"I know . . . I know." Mrs. Somers wept.

When we reached Geary Street, it was packed

with refugees. Mr. Somers and Mr. McGregor set the tongue down to rest.

"This here's where we turn," Mr. Somers said. "Southwest about two miles is Golden Gate Park, after that the ocean. Lord willing, we won't be pushed in."

Edith shaded her eyes as she looked around. "Daisy, City Hall is to the east somewhere. It seems hopeless, but there's got to be a way to get there. Father might be waiting for us on the steps, if he's . . . if he's not . . ." She fell silent.

A moment passed, then she brushed wisps of hair out of my eyes. "Daisy, I know you're concerned for Molly, so you don't have to come with me this time. It's just that, suddenly, the idea of wandering around alone . . . looking for Papa alone . . . What if I can't find him, and then what if I can't find *you?*" Edith gave a nervous laugh, then bit her lip. Her eyes were moist.

"Let's stay together" was my quick reply. My heart soared as it had the first time she'd asked me to read aloud in her classroom. I was eleven then, and newly arrived from Carson Hill. My father knew Mr. Irvine from the mines and they had agreed I needed schooling and that I was old enough to earn my keep. I was given an alcove in the Irvines' attic, numerous chores, and late-night tutoring by a patient, soft-hearted Edith.

Now she was saying *she* needed *me*.

Mary Exa overheard us. "Any moment now Molly McGregor is going to be having her baby, and I'd like to be here for her, Edith. You can look for us later in the park. . . . Oh, your father is a lucky man to have a daughter like you!" She and Edith flew into an embrace. It was the embrace of friends, long and heartfelt.

"Be careful, please!" called Mary Exa when we wheeled away the buggy. Her sleeves billowed as she waved good-bye. There were so many people heading every which way I wondered how we would ever find each other in the park. I worried about Molly and I worried about Mr. Irvine. The chances of running into him seemed desperately slim.

We must have been near Chinatown. Several men reminding me of Charlie were watching the fire. They wore the same cotton tunics over loose pants, and dark cotton shoes. The fronts of their scalps were shaved, and their hair was oiled back into pigtails that hung to their waists. I saw no women.

I wondered if these men were like Charlie, with wives and children far across the ocean, living in

China. Because Charlie and his brother, Johnny Lee Sing, were not born in America, our government wouldn't allow their families to join them here. If they returned to the Orient to visit their families, they were forbidden to reenter the United States.

Edith had explained this law to me when I asked about Charlie's wife. She said it was an amendment to the Chinese Exclusion Act of 1882. Charlie and Johnny Lee Sing, who was Dr. Willy's cook, had sailed to our land of opportunity with high hopes, and now they would never see their families again. Boys who had left China before marrying age were doomed to a life of bachelorhood because another law wouldn't let them wed non-Chinese.

Tears welled up when I thought of Charlie. I suddenly wanted to get word to Mokelumne Hill that we were safe.

A big shock on the second day caused several injuries and one woman, while getting dinner, was killed by a chimney falling through the roof and striking her.

Chapter 13

"HOW'S CITY HALL?" Edith called to people passing in the street. Her voice was getting hoarse and there was an urgency in her manner. She kept a hand on the buggy's hood so we wouldn't lose each other. A minister approached us. His white collar was smudged with charcoal and his coat was torn at the shoulder, but he smiled at us warmly.

"Who is it you're looking for, my dear?" he asked. Edith explained about her father and our getting separated, trying not to cry between words. The minister glanced at the small Bible in his hands.

"I'm afraid much of our beautiful City Hall came down with that first quake." He seemed to be choosing his words carefully. "It is surrounded by flames as we speak."

Edith closed her eyes. Her hand grasped mine.

The minister moved closer to us. "Let's pray right now that you and your father are reunited safely."

"Yes, please."

We bowed our heads, and for the first time since our trip began, I felt a hint of peace.

Much later we found City Hall; it was indeed hidden by roiling clouds of black smoke. We turned away, no longer in a hurry.

"Daisy, where could he possibly be? Was he in the building when it started to burn? Maybe we should head back to the harbor. Maybe Papa's looking for us there. I just don't know. I don't know what to do. I don't know what to think . . ." Edith's voice broke.

She ran a few yards and grabbed a man by the

front of his coat. "Have you seen my father? Where is he? *Where is my father?*" She began sobbing when the man gently pushed her away.

I hurried over to her, but not knowing what to say, I just threw my arms around her as Mary Exa had. My head ached with wanting to cry.

For a moment we held each other, then we sat on a low wall. Ten minutes passed, our tears silent. Finally, Edith wiped her cheeks and looked at me.

"I'm hungry. I want a bath," she said.

"Same here."

"Well . . . Papa would want us to carry on, don't you think? Bath or no bath, I can certainly take some photos. Would you help me, Daisy?"

"Yes, ma'am!"

Aware that keeping busy would help calm Edith's fears, I helped her sort through her glass plates. Making sure no policemen could see us, we draped the tarp over the camera so she could duck underneath. I realized we had so far seen just one person with a camera, a young reporter, and he was being harassed by the authorities.

Edith taking a picture was an interesting sight: below the tarp was the slim form of a woman, her long red hair reaching to the waist of her skirt; her frayed hem swept over shoes so scuffed Mrs. Irvine would have scolded.

Perhaps it was this sight that drew the man on horseback. He was handsome, with curly brown hair and no hat. He didn't seem to be a soldier or policeman. His smile was radiant, even though two of his bottom teeth were missing.

"Howdy," he said to me.

"Hello."

Still under the drape, Edith pulled the tripod a few inches to the left, a movement that caused her to stumble.

The man slid out of his saddle and grabbed her elbow. I could see he was trying to help, but Edith must have thought he was trying to steal her camera. She shoved him off and emerged with a look of fury. Her hand was raised, ready to strike.

"You have some nerve, mister," she said.

He backed away. "Sorry, ma'am, I just didn't want you to fall."

"We don't need your help," Edith snapped. When she realized he was not leaving, she fixed a steely look upon him. I had seen Edith this way with the rough boys in class. She could be as stern as a preacher. "We have work to do, and it does not include having you breathe down my neck. Now, if you'll excuse me, Mister . . ."

". . . London. Jack London." He saluted.

Eyebrows raised, she nodded. "Jack London, eh? Charmed to make your acquaintance, Mr. London. I'm Beatrix Potter."

Edith moved her camera toward a row of houses, repositioned the legs of the tripod, and ducked under the tarp.

The man was laughing. He looked at me with a shrug of his shoulders. From his jacket he pulled out a pocketknife and a pencil, which he sharpened with three strokes of the blade. Still grinning, he opened a small notepad and began writing against the flat part of his saddle.

I heard the shutter click. Edith slowly backed out from the drape. She watched the man write. It seemed she was studying the cut of his jacket and his fine leather cowboy boots. His denim pants were clean but dusty, and the blue scarf around his neck brought out the blue of his eyes. He had the assurance of someone who is well rested and who has not missed any meals.

"What did you say your name was?" she asked him.

Smoothing a curl off his forehead, he just smiled. They looked at each other for a moment.

"All right then," she said, "where was Buck born and how did he get to the Klondike?"

"California. He was stolen."

"What was the name of his master in Alaska, the one who was kind?"

"John Thornton."

Edith drilled the man with questions, once again the schoolteacher. The man was a star pupil. Much amused, he answered each question correctly and as briskly as she had asked.

Finally, she stopped. She held out her hand and introduced herself, looking at him with embarrassment.

"Mr. London, I owe you an apology. We've been without sleep for so long and with all that's happening . . . please forgive my rudeness. I have read *Call of the Wild* twice. It's good. I also was quite taken with *White Fang*. Someday they will be classics, I'm sure."

He laughed good-naturedly. "I enjoy a little repartee once in a while, Miss Irvine."

"Well then," she said, "are you going to put this earthquake into one of your stories now?"

"Never," he said, shaking his head. "I'll never write a word about it. What's the use trying? One could only string big words together and curse the futility of them."

For nearly two hours the three of us watched the fire. He told us he had left yesterday afternoon from his Glen Ellen ranch. A stone barn he was having built had crumbled because, as it turned out, the contractor secretly used flimsy material. Mr. London managed to board a train at Santa Rosa. After many delays alongside twisted rails and toppled water tanks, he arrived in San Francisco. His horse was a rescued runaway.

I could see that Mr. London and Edith were very much alike. They shared a passionate curiosity for people and events, and they both had wanted to study this disaster. Their talk of adventure reminded me of the *Susanna*.

"I bet there are other ships sailing for Australia this week," I told them. "Maybe your father will find us and we can transfer the tickets to another voyage. It's possible. I know it is."

Edith and Mr. London exchanged a look I didn't understand. Suddenly there was a shuddering under our feet. Mr. London's horse reared in panic. He was able to grab its reins before it bolted. My heart pounded. I was so shaken I felt if I started to cry, I would never stop.

The sound of a man screaming rose from the wobbly house in front of us. He ran outside, hysterical. Through the doorway we could see a distraught child with a plate of food. Stew dripped onto his bare feet.

"Mama!" he wailed.

Sixteen little babies were born in the [Golden Gate] Park the day after the quake and one woman had triplets.

Chapter 14

NEIGHBORS RUSHED IN to help the family. My heart ached. Seeing the child cry for his dead mother was more than I could bear. Images from the past hours pounded in my head: the bassinet, the horses . . .

I feared that at any moment another quake would knock me down and I, too, would be buried alive.

With that thought my knees buckled. I lay in the dirt, not caring that it muddied my mouth as I sobbed.

"Daisy!" Edith cried, bending near. "Are you all right?"

I felt strong arms lift me. Mr. London carried me to his horse and gently sat me in the saddle. He removed his scarf. After wiping my face with it, he tied it around my neck in a loose knot.

"You've seen more than anyone should see in a lifetime, young lady," he said. "Tell me where you're headed and I'll escort you."

In a few minutes I had stopped crying. Edith tried to comfort me by stroking my hand, but still a heaviness gripped me, as if a thousand sobs waited to burst forth.

Even though I was well acquainted with horses, I was nervous on this one. Its every step felt like a jolt to me. And what if it became frightened and took off running? How would I ever find Edith again?

I was too exhausted to think further on this. Instead, I complimented myself on my appearance. At least my skirt was wide enough so I could ride without too much petticoat showing. My high-laced shoes stuck out above the stirrups.

Mr. London led his horse through the crowd, with the reins over his shoulder. He and Edith talked, sometimes stopping to carry our buggy over the rocky path. She often looked back at me, then would smile when she saw I was all right.

From my perch I had a better view of the city than I'd had on foot. Black clouds swirled over the hills. I could see a hospital being evacuated with its many rescue carts and ambulances choking the street. Flames curled out of the gaping windows like tongues. Wind swept smoke our way, and soon ash began to fall like a soft gray snow.

Through the haze we finally saw Golden Gate Park. There were hundreds, maybe thousands, of people with such an assortment of wagons, tents, and baggage, I almost started to cry again. How would we find our friends? How would we ever find Mr. Irvine?

When Edith and Mr. London began to say good-bye, I lifted my knee over the horn of the saddle and made the most awkward departure from a horse a lady ever could. The instant my feet hit the ground my skirt caught on the horn, lifting it and my petticoat over my head. Several families along the curb were introduced to the sight of my bloomers, pink lace and all.

Seeing my predicament, Edith hurried over to unhook me. I was too humiliated to speak. A true gentleman, Mr. London kept his eyes on my hair until my dress was restored to order, then he gave me a brotherly handshake.

"May we meet again, Daisy Valentine."

He turned to Edith. With a slight bow, he kissed her hand, then swung onto his horse. Soon he was riding through the crowded street toward the harbor.

"He's almost as handsome as my pa," I said with a sigh. "I'd marry Mr. London in a minute."

Edith's eyes lingered on him. "I know what you mean, Daisy."

The bright yellow wheels of the popcorn wagon caught my attention. It was parked alongside a hedge. A blanket hung from the roof down to the bushes, forming a lean-to. On the wagon step Mr. Somers and Mr. Westlake sat with the eldest McGregor boy between them, trying to console him. They all seemed worried about the activity under the awning.

Mr. McGregor was nervously trying to keep his two youngest sons from bothering their mother, who was lying on her side, breathing heavily. Mary Exa sat so she and Molly could clasp hands. When Mrs. Somers saw us she threw up her arms in relief.

"Thank the Lord you two are here," she said. "Our poor Molly is having a most awful time getting this baby born. We sent Mrs. Westlake to look for a midwife and some water."

A loud gasp escaped from Molly's parched lips. Her face turned red as she tried to sit up. With a scurry, Mrs. Somers knelt. Edith and I instinctively spread our skirts to screen Molly from onlookers. With wide eyes I watched Mrs. Somers reach under Molly's smock.

"Come on, darlin'," she told her. "One more push and its shoulders'll be out."

In another instant there was a squalling little cry, and Mrs. Somers pulled a slippery newborn into her arms. It was wet, with something white, like lanolin, on its skin. A rubbery pink cord was connected to its stomach. I had never seen such a sight. Immediately, I felt protective toward the baby.

In no time Mary Exa had severed the cord with a sharp stone. She diapered the baby with a dish towel, wrapped it in a plaid flannel shirt, and tied the sleeves securely around its tiny body.

Molly named her daughter April Francisco McGregor. A midwife who later visited told us she had attended nine births by eleven o'clock that morning, and at least seven more women were in labor. Presidio Park had already seen twenty-three babies born. She pronounced April Francisco reasonably healthy, then told us to keep Mrs. McGregor from getting chilled. When we found more water, we were to sponge them both clean.

Before the midwife left, she looked at the infant with tired eyes.

"God sends earthquakes and babies, but I wish in His mercy He wouldn't send them together."

Poor Mrs. S[omers] is a little bit fatter than I, and after walking and standing all day she could not even turn over at night and had to be rubbed and lifted out of bed and exercised before she would begin a new day.

Chapter 15

"MAY I HOLD HER?" Edith asked, peeking into the tent.

"Aye, but the lassie's wet as a mop, my friend."

"Don't worry, Molly. We'll fix her right up." Edith emerged from the lean-to with April Francisco cradled in her arm.

"Look, Daisy, how sweet she is, and tiny. Have you ever changed a baby?"

"Never."

"Oh dear . . . neither have I." She looked around our campsite, then gestured toward a pile of clothes next to a trunk. "Well?"

Soon we had diapers from blue linen napkins, fastened with a brooch on one side and a twist of yarn on the other. We made a shirt by poking holes in a tea cozy, then fashioned a hat from a wool sock. The day was chilly, despite the infernos blazing through the streets east of us. Golden Gate Park was edged by windblown surf. We had been outside for so long, the damp air from the ocean seemed uncomfortably cold.

We listened, horrified, to Mr. Somers and Mr. Westlake argue over headlines in a *Berkeley Reporter* brought over by ferry. Wednesday's late edition had dreadful news: a global earthquake had wiped out Los Angeles and buried Chicago and New York under twenty feet of water. Seattle was burning worse than San Francisco.

If this was fact, maybe Pa wasn't as safe as I'd thought. At the time of the quake, he had probably been inside the Golden Girl mine. Did the timbers collapse . . . had he been buried alive? Was Mrs. Irvine all right?

I was frightened by what Mr. Westlake continued to read: every waterline in San Francisco was broken, and the sewers were leaking. All telephone and telegraph lines were down. Agnews Insane Asylum was in ruins, with 117 dead, including doctors and nurses. Inmates who had escaped were so wild that when captured they were tied to trees with sheets. Looters of saloons were becoming too drunk to run from the flames, so many died.

Could Mr. Irvine have been struck by falling bricks or trapped by fire?

Finally, they read news about the Somerses' friend, Chief Sullivan: he had been crushed by a wall while trying to rescue his wife and was not expected to live.

"I'm sorry, Harold," said Mr. Westlake. "Maybe it ain't true, maybe it just ain't true."

Mr. Somers laid the newspaper on his lap and gazed toward the fires. "Gosh," he said. "I can't hardly believe it. Why, just the other evening—it was a lovely evening; the stars were out, as I recall—they strolled by for some shortbread and blackberry jam. The poor missus."

Edith smiled at the men sympathetically, then she gave me a worried look. "Now I'm concerned about Moke Hill, aren't you, Daisy? If Mother's not hurt she must be frantic about us and Father. She would absolutely . . . perish . . . if she lost us." Edith took a deep breath. It seemed she had more to say.

"Holding this baby reminds me of my brother," Edith continued.

"Bob, you mean?"

"No . . . Clinton."

"Clinton?" I didn't know she had another brother.

"He was two when he died," Edith said. "Two years, two months, and fourteen days, to be exact. I was almost five. How I adored him. There was an accident, I guess you'd call it." Edith looked down at April Francisco, who slept soundly, warm in her little hat, but pale. Her lips were bluish. *Weren't babies supposed to be pink?*

Edith brushed her finger against the baby's cheek and gave her a motherly smile. I felt honored that she—my schoolmistress and employer—was talking to me as if I were her friend. She didn't seem bothered that I was so much younger.

"Our maid Lill, she was about your age, Daisy—

an orphan. Well, she was bathing Clinton in a tub by the stove. She'd forgotten a towel so she ran upstairs. But by the time she returned, Clinton was underwater. Just like that.

"Mother was never the same. They buried Clinton in the San Andreas cemetery on a sunny spring morning. There were so many robins singing I thought a chorus of angels had landed. Father planted a rosebush. After all these years, he still takes meticulous care of that grave."

A breeze lifted Edith's hair off her shoulders, revealing her graceful neck. "There's a poem," she continued. "It's carved on his headstone—sometimes I hear Mother singing it:

"Sleep on in thy beauty, thou sweet angel child,
By sorrow unblighted, by sin undefiled.
Like the dove to the ark, thou hast flown to thy rest,
From the wild sea of strife, to the home of the blest."

I didn't know what to say. Now I understood why Mr. and Mrs. Irvine made so many trips to San Andreas, the little town eight miles south of Mokelumne Hill, and why they were so solemn upon their return. It was odd, but I felt closer to Edith—maybe because now I knew we shared something. Her life of privilege hadn't been as perfect as I'd thought.

I wondered if this was why she hadn't photographed the crushed bassinet we saw earlier.

Mrs. Somers joined us in the grass with baby Timothy, who looked plump and robust compared to Molly's newborn. She rubbed her swollen feet. There was dirt on her chin. "How I'd love a hot bath and a shampoo about now," she said. "It hurts to sit, it hurts to walk, and my back ain't used to this hard ol' ground."

Yes, we agreed. Edith and I were so worn out that the longer we sat, the better we felt. I could see the danger in this: soon we would be so secure with our new family, we might delay trying to find her father.

As we rested in the sunshine, I thought about Mrs. Irvine. Maybe losing Clinton was what made her jaw so tight. Maybe she was harsh with me because I reminded her of Lill.

I was surprised to find myself thinking about Mrs. Irvine without the loathing I'd felt before. Something had happened to me this morning when I'd seen Molly McGregor in labor. At the moment she'd given birth, a thought had unfolded inside me and was growing.

My own mother had done this for me. Though she had died when I was just a few hours old, I knew she had loved me. This knowledge gave me a feeling of tenderness for all mothers and now, especially, for Mrs. Irvine.

The second day we stayed on the street most all day, sitting out in the sunshine and watching the fire sweep over old familiar spots. No one was allowed to leave or come into the city, which by that time was under martial law and no one but soldiers had authority.

Chapter 16

I WOUND THE KNOB on the top of my watch. It was almost one o'clock in the afternoon, Thursday. Sunshine began to warm us as we rested among our belongings. We still had not slept.

Every minute new clusters of refugees entered the park, searching for friends but, instead, finding friendly strangers. On one side of us, beneath a pine tree, was a large Italian family. I counted nine children, all barefoot. The father, Mr. Mirabito, told us they had tried to board a ferry but were turned away by soldiers.

Maybe Mr. Irvine had also been turned away and he, too, would find his way to this park. Edith and I were more watchful now, with this new hope.

Reporters from around the country who had made it as far as San Francisco's harbor were forbidden to dock, particularly those with cameras. When we heard this, Edith glanced at the buggy hidden under the lean-to.

"Mr. Somers," she asked the large man, "who is behind this no-photograph rule? I'm puzzled, especially because I know I can't be the only one with a camera."

"Me and Mr. Westlake was wondering that very thing, dear. Meantime, with all the guns going off hither and yon, you're smart to hide that equipment of yours."

Mr. Westlake scratched under his white beard. "Could be Mayor Schmitz and his cronies are embarrassed their city is such a mess. Why, the quakes in 'sixty-five and 'sixty-eight made so many houses fall that folks were beginning to wonder if maybe they should build stronger walls on ground that won't sink." He winked at Edith and lowered his voice.

"But if buildin' inspectors don't inspect and mayors don't make sure they're inspecting, well . . ." Mr. Westlake hunched his shoulders in a mock question.

"But that was a lot of years ago," I said.

"Oh, there've been honest mayors since then, my dear, good men who've helped our beautiful city become what it is." Mr. Westlake settled on the grass against the wagon wheel to stretch his legs. He looked like a respected statesman with his snowy hair and beard, surrounded by younger faces. The noise in the park made us draw near to listen.

"Why, just Tuesday night, officials were meeting. They was discussing all the illegal doings of Mayor Schmitz, charming as he is, and what charges to file against him."

Mr. Somers sat down heavily next to his friend. He knew this story and his jaw moved with his wanting to tell it. But he let his elder continue.

"Now then," Mr. Westlake chuckled, "this big ol' quake has postponed Mr. Schmitz's problems and interrupted everything else, hasn't it?"

Interrupted was right. I tried to imagine how Edith felt. Just two days ago she had been looking forward to a feather bed in a Paris hotel where royalty stayed. Her prints of Yosemite were to have been one of the few American exhibits and probably the only ones by a woman. And *I* was to have been the best photographic assistant in Europe, possibly the whole world.

Now I felt ashamed of myself. Edith gave no hint of sharing my deep disappointment. Her concerns were for her father, her mother, Molly, and the new baby.

Edith and I set out with the jug and watering can, this time without the cameras. Mary Exa remained behind to help with the four little boys and Molly's new baby. She hooked a bright red shawl onto a stick and planted it atop the popcorn wagon, where it waved in the sea breeze. Now we'd have no trouble finding our friends.

My shoes rubbed miserably on blisters that had become raw. Every step hurt. My pain was quickly forgotten, though, when we reached Broderick Street.

Fire fighters, one by one, were staggering toward the park. Most dropped from exhaustion at the curb. They lay as if dead, their yellow rubber coats, faces, and hands blackened like chimney sweeps'.

Several of us rushed to help them. Edith and I rolled one man up to the grass, as he was too heavy to carry. His hair was singed. When we tried to remove his coat I was horrified to see the sleeves had melted into his arms. A stringy rag hung from his wrist. When I tried to unwrap it, we realized it wasn't a rag. It was skin.

"Please!" Edith cried. "Someone help us!"

She cradled the man in her lap, one hand raised as if wanting to stroke his hair but afraid she would hurt him. His cheeks and forehead were blistered, and there was a black crust on his chin and nose.

"Daisy, I don't know what to do." She squeezed her eyes shut and took a deep, shuddering breath. Gagging from the horror of it, I turned away and vomited into the grass.

Two nurses approached us. Their smocks were muddied white, and each had her name above a pocket, embroidered in blue. Louisa Linscott, M.D., and Margaret Mahoney, M.D. They were not nurses. I had never heard of women being doctors.

One pulled a long needle out of a black bag. The other opened a vial of clear liquid. After filling a syringe, Dr. Margaret gave our fireman a shot. If he felt the sting of the needle, he didn't show it.

"What are you giving him?" Edith asked.

"Strychnine."

"Strychnine?" I gasped.

"That's poison," said Edith.

"Yes," said Dr. Louisa. "But not enough to hurt him. It'll just numb the pain from his burns and give him a boost of energy so he can go back out. We're doing it for all the firemen."

Edith and I exchanged looks of disbelief as the doctors moved along the line of prostrate men, using their needle on each.

"What's going to happen to them?" I asked.

Edith shook her head. "I don't know," she said. "Daisy, I can't sit here anymore. . . . I can't. These poor men. I feel so *helpless."* She unbuttoned her waistcoat, rolled it into a ball, and gently slid it under the man's head as she moved him out of her lap.

We watched doctors and nurses examine the fire fighters. Someone used a pocketknife to carefully slit away the coats. A woman, round and heavy with an unborn child, spread her shawl over the fellow Edith had held. Mothers who had been quieting their children came with blankets. The weary men were tenderly covered and watched over.

"God bless San Francisco's firemen," said an el-

derly man who resembled Mr. Westlake. He carried
a bottle of wine among the men, tipping it to their
parched mouths. "They've had no sleep or food or
comfort, and there's not a drop of water in our poor
city. If you ask me, they deserve medals."

They do not report the worst things as it injures future prospects here—and they do not want outsiders to know how bad it is. . . . The doctors will not give correct lists of the dead and injured, and no one will ever know the true state of affairs.

Chapter 17

WE WANDERED THROUGH Golden Gate Park. Its acres of grass were occupied by so many oddly formed shelters, it reminded me of a mining camp. There were the noises of children and of adults talking, the clink of hammers as men pounded tent stakes. Groups of strangers gathered around cooking fires, sharing chunks of bread and whatever bits of food had been salvaged. Those who had water made tea from dandelion greens.

A piano that had been pushed through the streets was surrounded by clapping, stomping people. I recognized the tune "There'll Be a Hot Time in the Old Town Tonight" and thought someone must have a dark sense of humor. As we came closer we saw two ladies sitting sassy-like on top of the piano. On an upturned crate perched a man whose fingers raced across the keys better than those of any saloon player I'd ever seen.

A fiddler joined the crowd, and soon someone was clicking along with spoons and another was drumming an empty coffee can. An elderly man and woman danced to the popular "Pony Boy Ponce."

I set to tapping my foot—the familiar music made me feel safe. Had there been an earthquake after all? Was San Francisco really burning?

After several songs, Edith led me toward a circle of shrubs. A crudely painted sign said Ladies Only. We followed a path to a narrow open trench. It smelled worse than an outhouse on a hot summer day. Edith and I had no choice but to imitate the ladies in front of us, much to my embarrassment.

When we were through, we saw some boys running by. One held two bullfrogs; the other had a large white bird in his arms. It was limp. It was also dripping wet.

"That looks like a swan."

Edith's face lit up. "It is!" she said.

"But . . . it's dead, I think."

"It may be dead, but a few minutes ago it was swimming. Daisy, I've been so fatigued, I completely forgot. There are several ponds in this park, and even a lake."

"If there's a lake . . ."

"Yes, yes, there's water!" Edith lifted the jug into the air as if making a toast.

I unlaced my shoes and waded beyond the bank to fill the watering can and jug. My dress got soaked from the knees down because I did not want to hike it high like a hussy. I kept my hat on.

After splashing the dust from my face, I scooped a drink with my hand. It had a fishy taste, but it soothed my throat. It was wonderful.

Wonderful, that is, until I noticed two mothers around the cove. Each was dipping a bawling infant into the water to wash its tiny bottom. Another woman was rinsing diapers, scrubbing them with sand, then hanging them over bushes to dry.

I swallowed hard. The thought of drinking unclean water made me queasy, but it *was* water and it *would* keep us alive. Edith held our pitchers while I dried my sore feet with my sleeves. As I laced my shoes we saw something else.

In the center of the lake several swans glided in the waning sunlight, oblivious to someone swimming their way. I was horrified yet not really surprised when, in one swift movement, the swimmer grabbed a bird's neck, wrung it with both hands, then began pulling for shore.

Hunger twisted in my belly. But it was some comfort knowing others were hungry, too. I was nearly ready to eat a swan myself.

Edith and I started for the popcorn wagon. The park was immense, but soon we sighted Mary Exa's red flag and the bright yellow wheels. As we walked, we saw many dripping ducks and geese, also some frogs, being brought to the cooking fires. Already there was an aroma of roasting meat.

Thursday's sunset was bleeding into the ocean when we finally reached our friends. Our water was gratefully received, first offered to the small boys and the nursing mothers. A saucerful was saved for Mrs. Westlake's sullen cat. No one mentioned the fishy taste, and I said nothing about the diapers.

Molly took only a small sip, then rolled onto her side. Her high color meant fever, but none of us dared say so. I soaked Mr. London's scarf in what was to have been my portion of water, then sponged her neck, face, and wrists. Her skin was hot. Edith massaged Molly's bloated feet.

Mr. McGregor was haggard with worry. He was trying to play with his sons but instead would stare over at his wife.

Meanwhile Mr. Somers and Mr. Westlake were discussing their sightseeing tour along Valencia Street, where a hotel had collapsed like a telescope. People on the fourth story stepped out their windows to the sidewalk.

"It sank like a rock in quicksand," Mr. Westlake told us, shaking his head sadly. He stroked his white beard as he spoke.

"Well sir," said Mr. Somers, "what d'you expect when they build on swamps? Mercy, those poor folks! Trapped, then drowned. I blame the Bricklayers' Union. If they hadn't been so worried about their jobs, the city coulda built with reinforced concrete and those walls would be standing today, I bet."

"That's right, Harold." Mr. Westlake pulled out his pipe. He had no tobacco, but still he sucked on the stem. After a moment he took it from his mouth.

"What I'm having trouble figurin'," he said, "is why that doctor told us hardly any people died. I know for a fact the Valencia Hotel rented rooms to dozens of fellas, *dozens*. Are we supposed to believe they all happened to be out of town visiting relatives when the earthquake hit?"

All night the fire raged and all night the earth shook from the great explosions of dynamite, block after block went down and many people were ordered to leave their homes so quickly they saved nothing more than they wore. It was sad to sit here and listen.

Chapter 18

IT WAS THURSDAY NIGHT. Throughout the park people gathered around small fires for warmth and to console one another. The good smell of coffee drifted our way. How hungry I felt. We shared the remaining shortbread and oranges, but our stomachs were still empty.

We were exhausted. I was worn out from walking and searching. I wanted to find Mr. Irvine, but I needed rest more. I was safe with friends and I wanted nothing more than to sleep.

Under the lean-to Mrs. Somers settled next to Molly, who was still silent with fever. Their infants were nestled between them for warmth. The men lounged nearby, talking quietly. Mrs. Westlake lay in her husband's lap. I stretched out in the damp grass, using a discarded boot as my pillow.

Too weary to move, I closed my eyes. There were voices and the thunderous booms of dynamite. My mind drifted dreamlike. It seemed I was in the attic back home, lying on my cot, a fierce storm outside. I felt my cat jump on me, then walk along my arm. I tried to pet him.

Cold little paws touched my hand. They walked over my stomach, along my leg, then back again. Bad Boy was nervous tonight, I thought, maybe from the thunder.

His whiskers tickled my neck. When he began sniffing my mouth I tried to brush him away. It was his tongue on my chin that finally woke me. My eyes flew open. I was not at home, and this was not my kitty.

Perched on my chest was the largest rat I'd ever seen. Its sloped chin was black like the rest of its body, and its tail was thick as a possum's. Its whiskers looked silvery in the firelight.

I held my breath. There was something moving down by my ankle and something else nosing its way under my dress.

More than anything I wanted to scream, scream until my voice gave out, but I knew if I did I might lose my mind completely. Instead, I eased my hand up to my head, grabbed the boot, and flung it down on the lump inside my skirt.

This prompted the rat on my chest to leap into the shadows. I scooted backward, kicking something away from my legs. It lay motionless, black and horrible as the other one. It was as big as my old tomcat.

I turned to the sound of screaming. Mrs. Somers was flailing under the tent, hysterical. She held both wailing infants as she tried to crawl out. Two large rats circled her knees. Another waddled over Molly's lap.

The men gave angry shouts as they stomped and kicked at the dark creatures. There were rats everywhere, rushing out of the bushes and rubble, fleeing the burning city. Edith and Mary Exa stood on a trunk and pointed frantically to the popcorn wagon.

"Daisy, the boys!"

I saw the little McGregors inside, curled together like puppies. Pacing back and forth along the rim was one of the rats. I threw my boot, knocking the rat to the ground. The boys didn't awake.

Everywhere people were beating the grass with sticks, pans, coats, anything. Our campsite was in turmoil as we tried to comfort each other, most of all to calm the distraught Mrs. Somers and Molly, who was unable to sit up. For the longest time they both wept, and, though their babies were unharmed, they kept checking their tiny fingers and toes.

Now that San Francisco was broken wide open, its lowliest citizens were homeless, too. Cockroaches and rats were searching for new nests just like the rest of us.

No one went back to sleep. We sat closer to each other, more alert. Even though it was after midnight, the blazing city cast such a glow I could read the newspaper Mr. Somers held.

I watched with longing as Edith and Mary Exa brushed each other's hair as they talked. Though they'd only met two days ago, they already cared for one another in the easy, comfortable manner of bosom friends.

With practiced hands Mary Exa swept her own

hair up in a twist, pinned it in place, then put on her hat. Edith's hair hung loose over her shoulders like a shiny red cloak. When she saw me watching, she smiled and moved closer.

"May I?" she asked, reaching to undo one of my combs.

Yes, I nodded. For several luxurious minutes Edith brushed my hair. How good the brush felt on my aching scalp. How good it felt to be part of her caring.

When she was done, Mary Exa knelt behind me to braid. I liked the way she coiled it up with combs, even though I couldn't see myself in a mirror. Edith retied the ribbon on my hat and bent the brim to curve down a little over my eyes, like Mary Exa's. The small personal rituals made it easier to bear our discomfort and the dismal surroundings.

We continued to stare at the flames. Every few minutes the air exploded with the sound of dynamite. Ash and cinders drifted onto us, coating our faces and clothes. I held Mr. London's scarf over my mouth and nose to keep from choking.

Mary Exa told us about her job as a stenographer at the *San Francisco Bulletin*. The publisher, Fremont Older, was her boss.

"When I was a girl in Louisiana I heard so much about the Wild West I just couldn't wait to get out here and see for myself. Never did I expect this much excitement," she said, sweeping her arm toward the fire. "Nor did I expect so many shady stories about our Mayor Schmitz. I am interested to hear Mr. Older's opinion on this dynamiting, because it appears to be making the fire larger, not smaller."

As we talked, more families straggled into the park, having been forced at gunpoint to leave their homes. Edith looked for familiar faces, asking if any knew the whereabouts of Thomas Irvine. Many were too distraught to answer.

"They wouldn't let me bring my wedding album," one lady wept as she fell into a stranger's arms.

One of the newcomers was a hollow-faced woman in a torn dress. Her hair fell in matted curls. To anyone who would listen she held out an oval frame. When she reached us, we saw it was a photograph of a little girl about five years old with blond ringlets and round, happy cheeks.

"Have you seen this child?" she asked us in a voice edged with panic. "Her name is Lucy. I've looked and looked, but I can't find her. . . . . I can't find her anywhere. . . . I . . ."

Without thinking, I rushed to embrace this mother. She was my height and frail as a bird. When our eyes met she broke into great, heaving sobs. So desperate were her cries, Edith helped us to the grass. For the longest time we three clung to each other.

$\mathcal{M}$rs. Somers and I got out and walked the streets about four in the morning wishing it was daylight, and we found everyone out walking or lying on the pavement wrapped in bedding. It was a most uncann[y]ing sight I assure you and a terrible roaring fire in the distance.

Chapter 19

AT FOUR O'CLOCK in the morning Mrs. Somers and Mary Exa began the long hike for Presidio Park, while Edith and I headed toward the ferry building. With four of us searching, perhaps we'd be able to find Mr. Irvine. Mrs. Westlake stayed with Molly. We were relieved her fever had gone down.

The streets were cluttered with abandoned carts,

sewing machines, and odd pieces of furniture, a piano here and there. One man slept on a velvet couch, his hat on his chest, his jacket draped over a graphaphone. Three Chinese men had set up cooking fires and painted a sign that said Restaurant Open for Business.

It was the middle of the night, yet there were so many people wandering around it could have been noon. I heard several foreign languages, which made me laugh at myself. Just four days ago my dream had been to see the world and all its people. I was living my dream all right—the only difference was I hadn't left California.

Edith and I walked slowly, careful not to lose sight of each other in the crowds. I had no idea where we were or how we would reach the ferry building. Every tall, mustached man drew our gaze. We asked families about Mr. Irvine, then described the popcorn wagon so they would know where to find us if they had any news. People promised to help.

Near Mission and Third streets, we joined a group of rescuers. Among them were several policemen and, I was happy to see, Mr. London. They were trying to free a man whose legs were pinned under a wall. I looked up. Black smoke clouded the top of the building as it swirled downward. Any moment now it would engulf us.

"Somebody shoot me!" the man begged. "For the love of Our Savior, *please*. I don't want to burn." He wept loudly, his hands folded in prayer. *"Please."*

Edith grabbed my arm. "Oh, Daisy, this is horrible. . . . I can't watch." She turned away just as an older gentleman stepped forward with a pistol.

"God, forgive me," he yelled to the sky.

At the instant we heard the shot, a hot gust of wind blew our skirts against our legs. Heat seared my face as if we'd opened an oven. Flames were shooting up and around the corner where we stood.

"Run!" someone screamed.

We hiked our skirts, trying to hurry over the rubble. I tripped and fell. My chin hit a sharp stone.

A man on horseback rode to my side and slid to the ground.

"Come on!" Mr. London shouted. He lifted me to the saddle, boosted Edith up behind me, then swung up himself.

He kicked his horse into a gallop. It jumped over a twisted trolley track, then headed for the center of the street, where others were running. The three of us bounced awkwardly against the saddle. I grabbed the mane with one hand and the horn with the other, unable to hold onto my hat, which flew off in the wind. Edith hugged my waist.

A milk wagon, pulled by two panicked horses, bolted from an alley, passing inches in front of us. Our horse spooked and as it did, I tumbled to the ground. It reared, then burst into a run.

"Daisy!" Edith screamed. I could see the long tangle of her red hair as she turned to look at me. A flash of Mr. London's face showed disbelief. With a piercing horror, I realized they couldn't stop the horse.

The driver of the milk wagon slit the harnesses with his pocketknife, allowing his horses to escape down the smoky street. He ran, too. Hadn't he seen me? The wagon rolled to a stop, its heavy metal wheels missing my face by a breath. I struggled to get up but couldn't. My skirt was pinned to the cobblestones by a rear wheel.

"Help!" I screamed, but there was only the sound of a roaring fire. No one could hear me. From where I lay, I could see the running legs of men. It would be easier to die, I thought, than to hope one of them might rescue me.

I rolled side to side, desperately trying to free my skirt, but it wouldn't tear loose. A smoldering beam crashed into the rubble nearby, scattering embers by my face. A coal the size of a penny burned my sleeve.

Without thinking, I ripped away the buttons at my waist and crawled out of my skirt and petticoat, then out from under the wagon. I ran.

So intent was I on fleeing the fire, it was two blocks before I stopped, coughing and retching from the exertion. A crowd had gathered and I could hear voices crying for loved ones. I tried to catch a glimpse of Edith or Mr. London's horse but saw only strangers. When I bent over to catch my breath, my eyes fell on the white knees of my bloomers.

With growing embarrassment, I realized my nakedness. Without my heavy skirt and petticoat, my bottom felt bare. My legs were cold. I put my hands behind my back, then in front of me, then back again. Nothing could be worse than this: to be surrounded by men who could see me attired as only a husband should see his wife.

But there *was* something worse.

I was lost.

*The early morning light was dull and hazy and the deathly
still air very oppressive. I was filled with a peculiar feeling of horror and
helplessness which I shall never forget.*

Chapter 20

As I WANDERED ALONG the street, I realized men
were not staring at me after all. Perhaps it was like
"The Emperor's New Clothes." Everyone *knew* I was
undressed but, out of courtesy, no one let on. Still,
I feared drawing attention to myself, so I did not
yell for Edith or ask for directions.

I was so frightened that I no longer felt hungry.

My chin was bleeding, and my hands were scraped. The blisters on my feet hurt in a distant way. How would I find Edith? How would I ever get back to the popcorn wagon?

"My dear, can we help you?" a woman asked me. Some elderly ladies sat warming themselves around a fire. When I saw the kindness in their faces, I began crying, a quiet, weary cry. There was no more strength to sob. I let them wrap a blanket around me and lead me to their circle. Someone pressed a mug with hot liquid into my hands and said, gently, "Drink."

It was only water, but it filled me with a wonderful warmth. Someone else put a piece of meat to my lips. It was juicy and tasted like chicken. Soon I was able to look up and see the women clearly. Grandmothers, I guessed. One unpinned her hat and approached me with her blanket.

Then, as if she were a seamstress and I a lady, she transformed her blanket into a skirt for me, fastening it with her two hat pins. It fell neatly to my ankles, with only a tiny bit of bloomer peeking out the side.

"There you are, my dear," she said.

My voice was hoarse, but I managed the words "Thank you."

The sky was beginning to lighten to a hazy gray. It was Friday morning. After one of the ladies cleaned the cut on my chin, they directed me to the street leading to the ferry building. I was hoping Edith may have gone there, as we had last planned.

I began walking. The landscape was a wilderness of ruin. People wandered around, picking through the rubble like stray animals. No one seemed to notice me. For some strange reason, this gave me courage. If no one knew I was scared, I could pretend I wasn't.

I reminded myself I had walked alone in the wilderness around the mining camps, and had even been lost once but managed to follow a river home. This street was like a river, I reasoned, and if I followed it toward the harbor, there the ferry building would be. Edith might not be there, but it was possible she might.

My cheerfulness astounded me. An hour earlier, my greatest fear was to have been away from Edith, lost. But now I *was* away from Edith and I *was* lost and it was not as horrible as I'd imagined.

By the time I reached the ferry building, I was no longer afraid. The harbor felt safe, even though fireboats were spraying the wharves and waterfront shanties.

When I stepped into the depot, my heart fluttered. Would I find her? Voices echoed under cavernous ceilings. There were cries of babies and older children. People lay on the tile floor, many bandaged with bloody rags. The variety of animals—dogs, cats, two ponies, someone's pet monkey—made it seem like a carnival. A parrot in a large iron cage squawked its distress.

Edith saw me first. The instant her arms flew around me, my bravery vanished and I began to weep. So did she. But soon we were laughing, such was our relief. Mr. London embraced both of us.

For nearly an hour we searched for her father, bending over sleeping faces, touching the shoulders of those awake. No one answered to the name of Thomas Irvine.

When Mr. London bade us farewell, I had a feeling we'd see him again. Edith and I began our long tramp back to Golden Gate Park, disappointed we hadn't found even a clue to the whereabouts of Mr. Irvine. Though the blisters on my feet stung like open sores and my chin ached, I was elated that Edith and I were together and about to return to our friends. It didn't matter that I felt ready to collapse from fatigue.

"Daisy?"

"Hmm."

"What do you think of Mr. London?"

"Well," I said, "I guess you could say he's handsome. He smells better than most of the fellas we've talked to."

Edith tightened her lips in an effort not to laugh. "I think he's positively extraordinary. He's worldly . . . clever . . . charming, no doubt about *that*. Did you see the way he comforted that little child? To top it, he's a marvelous writer."

"Is that all?"

"Mmm . . . no," she said, smiling.

Her hair swung at her waist as we walked, and her neck was erect. She must have felt herself blush because she laughed out loud.

"Stop looking at me, Daisy. *Honestly.*"

Now *I* had to laugh. Four years ago, I began living with the Irvines. I had seen Edith blush, and I had heard her laugh. I had even heard her discuss men. But this was the first time she'd done all three at once.

*The third day we went again to see the ruins. . . . It was a
terrible sight to see charred brick walls standing where such grand
structures once stood and such a wilderness of ruin.
It is horrible.*

Chapter 21

A MIST WAS RISING off the ocean. Waves surged
on the rocks below. The clamorous bark of sea lions
announced the sun breaking through the fog.

Mary Exa and Mrs. Somers greeted us as we returned. Disappointment and exhaustion showed on
their faces. They, too, had found no one answering

to the name of Thomas Irvine. For many minutes we sat in the damp grass, not speaking, too weary to voice our despair. No one seemed to notice the thin cotton blanket that had replaced my skirt.

When I realized that dew had soaked through to my bloomers, it gave me an idea. Running my hand over blades of grass, I soon had enough moisture to wet my mouth. Edith laughed helplessly.

"Daisy, I do declare!" she said. "What would we do without you?"

We must have looked like chimpanzees, bending and scooping everywhere and howling with the fun of it. The McGregor boys were delighted we'd thought up a game for them, and soon they were licking the metal rims of the wagon wheels. Moisture had pooled on rocks and also in the low part of the tent. We drank; we washed our faces and hands.

"There ain't enough for coffee," laughed Mr. Somers, "but by golly this is the best wake-up drink I've ever had."

"Here, here!" said Mr. Westlake.

Mrs. Westlake offered a drink to her cat in the cage. "I knew the Lord would provide if we were just patient."

———

The sun rose over the charred city in a sky stained brown. Smoke plumed in great black clouds, drifting upward in the still air.

We heard a bugle sport a happy tune, then a gong rang.

"It's over!" cried a voice, then two voices, then a chorus.

"It's over! The fire's out!"

We leaped to our feet, hugging each other. I swung Scottie McGregor into the air. Edith danced a jig with Mr. Somers. The Mirabitos threw hats in the air and rushed over. We embraced one another again and again.

"Thank God," Molly said from her bed. She raised herself on her elbow to look around. When she saw her sons playing, she smiled, then lay back down. Edith kneeled beside her to brush Molly's long auburn hair.

Throughout the park, bells clanged, bugles played, and there was the wonderful sound of singing. Music and dancing burst from the people, wild and joyous.

The McGregor family stayed in camp while we walked, my blanket now replaced by one of Mary Exa's skirts. The cobblestones were hot beneath our feet. Steam rose from the ashes. Lampposts had melted into shepherds' crooks. The rolling hills of San Francisco, once lush and grand, looked like the stubble of a man's beard. Street signs were gone, as were trees and other landmarks.

"Quite honestly, I don't know where we are," Edith said. "I *think* City Hall is that way." After all this time, there was only the slimmest of hopes that her father would be waiting for us there.

We took Edith's cameras with us, as a way to distract her while we searched. We also had a passenger for the buggy: baby Timothy. We folded down the hood so he could have a good view. He looked as rosy and well fed as the first moment I saw him.

When we came to a bread line, we agreed to split up for an hour or so. The Westlakes and Somerses were tired of walking, so they were happy to get loaves for us all. And they would rest.

The line wound along a broken sidewalk for three blocks. People waited patiently, some sat on bricks or boxes along the way. There was an air of community as folks talked to those around them. Servant girls were treated as graciously as matrons in pearls. Chinese men were not shoved aside.

Two barrels held scraps of blank white paper.

Some cigar boxes had been filled with pencil stubs. A worker in a dusty uniform promised people that if they wrote a message on one side and an address on the other, the United States Post Office would deliver the letters without stamps.

"We did not lose one bag of mail through all this," he yelled proudly. "Up where you get your bread, there's a tub on a wagon. Put your letters in that, and drop the pencils in the little box there for others to use. Let's show the rest of the world that San-Fran-cisco is back on her feet!"

Edith, Mary Exa, and I continued our search. I did not cling as closely to them as before, although I was careful that we stayed together. It felt wonderful to no longer be so afraid. Were others feeling this way, too?

We came to what must have once been a luxurious stone mansion. But now the roof had been dynamited off, and the windows were empty and black. A soldier stood guard outside against looters.

"Is this Claus Spreckels's home?" Edith asked him. "The sugar king's?"

"Yes, ma'am."

Edith kissed Timothy's forehead as she reached under his feet for her tripod. She handed me her cherry-wood camera. "I've had tea here. Mr. Spreckels is a friend of my father's," she said to us. Then she called to the soldier. "Is the family all right?"

"Fit as a fiddle," he said, "and with a brand-new baby, too."

"What?"

"Yes, Mrs. Spreckels gave birth right here in the front yard moments before the fire got here. They whisked her and the baby away in a carriage just in time." The soldier was so pleased to deliver such dramatic news he didn't seem to notice what Edith was doing.

While he recited other events, Edith adjusted her lens. The shutter clicked. She returned her camera, big as it was, to the buggy before he realized he'd had his picture taken.

"Now," she said, "maybe we can find City Hall. Maybe someone has seen my father."

It is a sad sight to see the dear old City Hall which required [twenty-four] years building a total wreck. . . . This calamity has brought everybody to a level—we are all equal sufferers and sharers of trouble—there is no distinction.

Chapter 22

SUCH CLIMBING UP and down hills. My legs ached, and my feet rubbed miserably in my stiff shoes. At last, from a distance, we could see City Hall. Or what was left of it.

Its cupola looked like an empty bird cage.

"It's destroyed," Edith whispered. She sat down

on the remains of a stone wall, then dropped her chin in her hands. She stared at the burned-out rubble. There were sightseers milling around, but no men conducting business meetings, none in gray traveling coats.

"Maybe your father was able to return to Stockton somehow," I said, wishing I could help her not worry.

Edith sighed. "I hope you're right, Daisy, but remember Father talking about claim jumpers at our mines? Well, all records and deeds, all *proof* that our family owns anything at all, were there." She pointed to the ruined City Hall.

"Surely there are records elsewhere?" asked Mary Exa in her soft drawl.

Slowly, Edith shook her head. Fighting back tears, she began setting up her camera, as if doing so would comfort her. I wasn't sure why she wanted to photograph something that caused her so much distress. Maybe she thought people would forget what had been lost if there were no pictures to remind them.

As we headed back to Golden Gate Park I thought about the Irvines and other families who had lost homes and money. This would change things in

Mokelumne Hill, but I wondered how. And what if Mr. Irvine was hurt or never to be found? What would happen then?

Edith cast a weary smile on Timothy, who had fallen asleep amid the lumps of camera equipment. His little blue socks had slipped off his heels. Gently she pulled them up, then covered him with part of the blanket.

When we neared the ocean, the cobblestones became slippery with moss and horse manure, which we had to step around every few feet. I wished men didn't spit anywhere they pleased, because we had to step around that, too.

At the entrance to the park, large planks of wood were nailed between trees. There was a barrel of blank paper with pencils. Hundreds of notes had been tacked up. We read as many as we could.

Edith searched for her father's name and those of other relatives and friends, then wrote a message of her own. After several more minutes of reading, she let out a whoop of excitement.

"Listen!" she said. " 'ATTENTION Adam Kern: Sarah and I are on way to Oakland camp will WAIT for you love TESS.' Daisy, that must be Tess Kern, Dr. Willy's sister. She and baby Sarah are all right!

We'll have to let Roland know immediately." When she mentioned Roland Willy's name, Edith looked down, then she looked at me.

"Are we going home?" I asked her.

She nodded. "Yes, Daisy, as soon as we can."

When we found the popcorn wagon about noon, the wonderful aroma of cooking greeted us. A juicy stew was bubbling over the fire. There were six long loaves of French bread.

"Trains have been arriving from all over the country," said Mr. Westlake, speaking with his mouth full. "Meat, potatoes, carrots, enough bread for everyone, medicine. Now we have proof the rest of the world hasn't been destroyed. Goes to show, ya can't believe everything you read in a newspaper."

Mrs. Somers handed me a tin cup of stew. "At least we have *something* to thank the army for," she said. "They've sent in tents and cots so we won't have to sleep on the damp ground too much longer. We're likely to get blankets all the way from New York City!"

As I started eating, Edith leaned close enough to whisper. "Daisy, I'm going to check on Molly. Hopefully her appetite has returned." She carried her cup to the tent.

I listened to the men discuss news gathered on their walks. Fire Chief Sullivan had died that morning from his injuries. Chicago wasn't underwater after all, and Los Angeles had only felt the earthquake, not expired from it. A group of San Franciscans, calling themselves the Citizens' Patrol, was roaming the ruins, serving justice to anyone who looked suspicious. They were undisciplined and untrained, and they had guns.

Mr. Westlake set his cup down. "My God," he said. "If anyone who wants to can carry a gun, we'll have neighbors shooting each other for the slightest offense." He stood up and left our circle, on the way bumping into a frantic Edith.

"Hurry, someone find a doctor!" she screamed.

"What . . . what's happened?" we cried.

But Edith had run back to the tent. I caught up to her as she unashamedly pulled down her petticoat and began wadding it up.

When I bent over to follow her under the awning, I saw the dark lake of blood.

*A rich man riding in his automobile was shot down
[by the police] for refusing to allow them to convey an injured man to
the hospital in his auto. . . . One man was shot for charging $1.25 for a
loaf of bread and many other things were done which
may never come to light.*

Chapter 23

MOLLY'S LIPS MOVED as if she were trying to speak.
We women knelt around her, filled with terror.
Mr. McGregor pressed his wife's limp hand to his
cheek, pleading with her to live.

The elder Mr. Westlake hurried off to find a
doctor, Mr. Somers his nervous companion.

April Francisco gave little mewing cries that in a

matter of seconds escalated to bawling. Molly tried to soothe her by touching her cheek, but when she did the baby's cries became more shrill. The tiny thing wailed with such desperation, hiccuping in between cries, I worried she would stop breathing.

"Goodness me," said Mrs. Somers. She swooped the infant into her arms, opened her blouse, and helped the tiny mouth find her nipple.

The noise stopped as suddenly as if someone had shut a door. Without thinking, Mrs. Somers had known what to do and so had that baby. Its contented suckling reminded me of a kitten's.

Now we turned to Molly. Edith was trying to stop the bleeding with her rolled-up petticoat. Mrs. Mirabito brought more cloth and a canteen. She poured enough water for us to sponge Molly's face and arms, for her fever was higher than before.

"Is she goin' t' be all right, mum?" Mr. McGregor asked. His face showed the panic I felt. All color was drained from Edith's cheeks as she tried to keep Molly awake.

When the two older men returned later, they were out of breath. "We found a doctor," Mr. Westlake explained, "but he was in an automobile. The police were driving him to a hospital. There're folks everywhere crying for doctors, I'm afraid."

Friday afternoon we stayed together. Mrs. Somers nursed Molly's baby every two hours and we all took turns diapering and rocking her. April Francisco was so small, she fit between my palm and elbow. The bluish tinge around her mouth was turning a healthy-looking pink.

By nightfall we had changed Molly's bed four times.

Stars glimmered over the dark ocean. Throughout the barren city we could see bonfires blazing in campgrounds. Music reached us on the cold evening breeze: piano playing and, from another direction, the soothing strums of a Spanish guitar.

We shared a fire with Mr. and Mrs. Mirabito and their nine children, meanwhile continuing to look in on Molly. As we ate our supper of bread and baked potatoes, I looked appreciatively at everyone: the Westlakes, Mr. and Mrs Somers and Timothy, Mary Exa and Edith, poor Molly, and the five other McGregors. We were such a large, noisy assortment of folks, I felt for the first time as if I belonged to a family. To think of leaving them was wrenching. The Irvine household would now seem so quiet, so empty.

All Friday night there were sounds of waves washing over the rocks and the occasional bark of a sea lion. With loose clothing, we made nests for the children. The adults settled into grassy crevices, talking quietly; some dozed.

The dampness made me shiver with cold. That and a growing fear Molly was slipping away from us made it impossible for me to sleep.

Everybody runs after the water wagon here. All milk and water must be boiled before using. The water is horrible—just full of green slime. I am so thirsty.

Chapter 24

HOW GLAD I WAS when the sky began to lighten in the east. Soon a tangerine sun rose above the hilly horizon and two horse-drawn wagons jangled into the park. Barrels of river water had been brought over by ferry.

Families started lining up with cups, pots, and

empty wine bottles, as patiently as they had for bread. By ten o'clock that Saturday morning, we had collected enough to have two pots heating, one for coffee and stew, the other for sponge baths.

Signs posted on trees warned people to drink water from the wagons only, and then only after it was boiled. No Digging, Danger of Typhoid, read another sign. An underground spring had been discovered, but the water had been contaminated by human waste. Wherever people had camped, the water was not fit to drink.

Mr. Westlake and Mr. Somers again set out in search of someone who could help Molly. Though her fever was high, she often strained for a glimpse of her children.

"They're all right," Edith kept reassuring her. "See, Scottie's playing leapfrog with Edward. Your daughter is with Mrs. Somers, see, by the fire? Just rest, Molly; we'll take care of them."

Mary Exa and I wandered through the park, looking for a midwife. We also called Thomas Irvine's name every few minutes, hoping, if nothing else, one of Edith's friends or cousins might respond.

Near the lake, a man had built a fire under a caldron propped up on bricks. The kettle came up to my waist, and the water inside boiled and steamed. Two faucets had been rigged. People waited in line with teapots and shaving mugs.

The man, a miner with a heavy beard, tended the flames. His canvas hat shaded his eyes and his rolled-up sleeves revealed muscular arms. Something about him made me step around the fire to get a better look at his face.

When he saw me staring at him, he slowly put down the pile of wood and straightened his shoulders.

"Either my tired eyes is playing tricks on me or the lady standing before me is none other than Daisy Valentine."

"Mr. Frank," I cried, rushing into his familiar arms. The stink of his shirt reminded me so much of my father I started to bawl.

"Now, now," he said. "What in tarnation are you doing in San-Fran-cisco, and all growed up at that? And how is that pa of yours?"

Between sniffles I told him the whole story, about Pa still mining Carson Hill, my being a servant for the Irvines, and my almost-trip around the world. When I finished, I wiped my nose on my sleeve, then remembered to introduce Mary Exa.

"Ma'am." He acknowledged her with a nod.

"Daisy, your pa must be mighty proud of you. It's been a couple, three years since I seen him—no, must be four 'cause I left Carson in 'oh-two. Does he visit you in Moke Hill?"

"Every month," I told him.

"Good, good. Say . . . I got something for you." He pulled a small pouch from his vest and put it in my hand.

"What's this?"

"Pepper," he answered. "Rats hate it. Sprinkle it on them long whiskers and they'll snort 'n sneeze and won't come back. I have lots of it." He patted his shirt pockets.

"There were rats here, too?" Mary Exa asked.

"Yes, ma'am. Thought they was little dogs or something, looking for a handout. When I seen they wasn't little dogs me and the fellas here kicked at 'em. Those rats took their time leaving, like they was invited guests. Not till I threw pepper in their beady black eyes did they disappear.

"Well, Daisy, you tell your pa hello for me," he said, lifting me into a hug. His whiskers scratched my face and his hair had the good smell of campfire smoke.

"Thanks for the pepper, Mr. Frank."

"You bet. Never thought I'd see the day when it

was worth more t' me than gold, but there you have it, another one of life's riddles."

Mary Exa and I returned to our campsite without having found a midwife. I was amused to see the McGregor boys chasing each other around the wagon, but when I saw the empty bed under the awning, my heart stopped.

"Where's Molly?" I cried.

Edith was sitting near the hedge. Her eyes were swollen and so full of sorrow, I knew the worst had happened.

Whole families are missing and the charred remains taken from the ruins cannot be identified. . . . In one place near Frisco, a cow is said to have been swallowed in an opening.

Chapter 25

MOLLY WAS BURIED at the edge of the park, among dozens of fresh graves. Mr. McGregor draped himself over the mound and wept. The rest of us were inconsolable, too. Even in the warm sunshine, I shivered from the wind off the sea.

Edith and I stayed behind after the others had helped Mr. McGregor carry his children back to camp.

The noise and activity around us overwhelmed me. Did no one stop, not even for death?

In the street behind us came a detail of men. Two soldiers with bayonets oversaw their work. One man carried a bucket of white powder that every few feet was sprinkled onto the ruins.

"Lime," a bystander offered. "Helps keep flies off the dead bodies."

Please. I didn't want to know about this.

Edith pointed to a haggard fellow in a torn tuxedo. He was slowly lifting bricks from the rubble and stacking them to the side. The bricks were so hot he kept blowing on his hands.

"Mr. Barrymore?" I whispered, remembering our first hours in San Francisco. She nodded.

But this was a different John Barrymore. Gone was the elegant posture. Somewhere during the past few days he had also lost his hat, ripped his pants, and grown a stubbly beard.

"Why are you making those men work?" I yelled to a soldier. My boldness surprised me.

He squinted as if he'd heard that question twelve times that morning.

"Lady," he yelled back, "when the volunteers start lining up I'll put down my gun. Till then, someone's got to take care of the dead, what's left of 'em."

With a morbid curiosity, I hiked up my frayed skirt to step over the rubble. "Mr. Barrymore?" I called, hoping the soldier wouldn't stop me.

The actor looked up with bloodshot eyes. He didn't seem surprised I knew his name.

"You were supposed to sail for Australia on Wednesday, remember?" I asked. "Aboard the *Susanna?*"

"So?"

"Well, I was wondering . . . will you still leave? Have you found another ship going across the Pacific?"

John Barrymore stood up straight, then he raised his chin. He held out his shovel as if it were an ivory-tipped cane and he a tap dancer. "Matter of fact, *mademoiselle,* my director has us sailing this P.M. on the SS *George Washington.* Why do you ask?"

Suddenly my confidence vanished. I didn't know why I'd asked, except that maybe I'd hoped our trip wasn't lost after all. Though we had no luggage or tickets or money, I knew I could work for our passage. I was used to cleaning up after people and eating scraps. It was a reckless idea, but Edith and I *could* travel.

But from the way she stood there, saying nothing, exhaustion in her eyes, I realized Edith needed to return home, that there was now something more important than my desire for adventure: family. Her mother would be desperately worried, and Edith would not sleep until she knew the fate of her father. And since I had promised to be Edith's companion, I would stay with her.

Then there was the matter of my own pa. I wanted to see if he was safe.

"Never mind," I finally answered; then, feeling embarrassed for him, I said, "It's nice of you to help out here."

A man nearby bent up from the bricks, with the loudest horse laugh I'd ever heard.

"Nice, my foot!" he roared.

Mr. Barrymore tossed a look of irritation at the man, then combed his hair with his fingers. "Oh, stop it, Clarence!" he said.

"Ladies, I'm the stage manager," the man said, "and I can tell you a few things about John Barrymore. It took an earthquake to get him out of bed before noon, it took a fire to sober 'm up, and it took the *Yoo*-nited States Army to make him work. *Nice,* my foot."

We returned to our friends. With the McGregor boys, Timothy, and little April, there was so much commotion that we didn't have time to sink into despair. But like the gray, windblown ashes drifting into camp, so did grief settle on us all.

Edith often held Molly's daughter; we both did when Mr. McGregor was busy tending his other children. The sight of this now-rosy baby brought smiles to everyone; even her heartbroken father was able to manage a smile.

Something else lifted my spirits: word spread through the park that packet boats would soon begin leaving for Sacramento and Stockton.

Home. Edith and I could go home.

$\mathcal{M}$rs. Somers and I were laughing yesterday about how
we slept in our clothes for weeks it seemed—too scared to even pull off
shoes, jackets or hats and I was glad I did not wear corsets as they
must have been very uncomfortable added to the already hard
beds on the pavements, etc., where we lay down to rest.

Chapter 26

SATURDAY NIGHT PASSED most slowly of all.
It rained.

The misery and the sloshing cold seemed unbearable as we huddled under our sopping blankets. By dawn, few had slept. Campfires smoked because of damp wood and, beyond, steam rose from the blackened city.

But the sun rose with such brilliance into a sky wide and empty of clouds that a feeling of cheer soon spread among us all. The ocean sparkled.

It was a glorious Sunday. Now that some of the crowds on the docks had thinned out, Edith and I were going to try for the noon boat. The captains were accepting whatever pay passengers could afford, and in many cases letting people on for free. Some had souvenirs to sell for passage, mostly items from Chinatown, the only place where looters were not being shot. Apparently, it was not a crime to steal from the Chinese.

Mr. McGregor handed me a gold stickpin with a tiny diamond on the tip. He gave Molly's silver pocket watch to Edith.

"Thank ye for helpin' Molly," he said. "She woulda wanted ye lassies to have these."

We gathered by the popcorn wagon. While the little boys and some other children played tag, Edith and I sorted through her glass plates. We carefully stacked their protective sleeves in the buggy, covered them with a shawl, then added the rest of her equipment.

There was grime on both cameras, and one leg of her tripod had been nicked by a falling brick. These we covered with someone's discarded coat.

We gave the blue lace-trimmed blanket to Mrs. Somers, for her to wrap around Molly's tiny daughter.

Now that I knew for certain we were not sailing for Australia, I was eager to return to Mokelumne Hill. I wanted to see Edith's photographs after she developed them in her darkroom. I wanted to see Charlie and Pa. And I wanted to find out if Mr. Irvine had made it to safety.

We did not speak about the dread we felt: what if bad news awaited us?

Mr. McGregor hugged us good-bye, then Mrs. Westlake embraced us.

"You are like granddaughters to me and Mr. Westlake," she said, crying. "Wherever our coffeepot is brewin', you're as good as home."

Mrs. Somers pulled each of us into her strong arms. "Soon as we have an address, girls, I'll write you. . . ." She wiped her cheeks with the hem of her apron, unable to finish. With her chin quivering, she put her half-eaten loaf of bread into our buggy.

"Oh, Mrs. Somers." Edith touched the woman's damp cheek. "I'll miss you. I'm so glad you'll be caring for her . . . for Molly's baby. As soon as any of you are able, will you come visit us in Moke Hill, please? All of you, anytime, come see us. If we can't fit in the house we'll just camp in the yard, won't we? For old times' sake." There was nervous laughter and tears.

Mary Exa clasped the handle of the buggy. "I'd like to walk you to the harbor," she told us.

"Not without me, you won't," said Mr. Somers. He put on his cap, then kissed his teary wife. "I'll see 'em safe to the boat, dear."

As we maneuvered through Golden Gate Park we heard the sweet sound of a cornet. The melody was so rich, so soothing, we stopped to listen. Hundreds of people gradually emerged from tents and lean-tos, gathering between the conservatory and tennis courts. Next to the cornet player was a white-haired minister standing on a crate. I nudged Edith. We recognized him as the one we'd talked to in the burning streets our first day here.

Voices sang in unison. I wasn't familiar with the words, but I knew them to be a hymn. When the chorus ended, the minister raised his arms to the blue sky, and as he did, every person sank to the grass.

"Lord," the minister began. His voice resonated as if we were in a cathedral. "Thy ways are beyond our understanding. Thou knowest the reason for this desolation and of our utter helplessness. . . . We call on Thee for help in the hour of our great need.

"Bless the people of this city, the sorrowing ones, the bereaved. Gather them under Thy mighty wing and soothe aching hearts this day."

Around me I could hear the sound of weeping. When the cornet began to play the long, peaceful notes of "Amazing Grace," my throat tightened. I knew these words, but I was unable to sing.

Mr. Somers removed his cap and looked heavenward. Tears streamed down his face. Two men nearby sobbed without shame. Mary Exa, Edith, and I held hands across our laps. So many feelings welled up inside me: sadness for the heartaches of those around us, and my own indescribable ache for Molly; I was relieved Edith and I were going home, but sad that going home meant leaving our new friends. In a way this made me saddest of all.

The crowd was still singing when we resumed our walk to the harbor. Four boats were loading up to journey through the San Pablo Bay and the Carquinez Strait. Two would branch north along the Sacramento River and two eastward, down the San Joaquin River to Stockton, our last stop before the stage.

Mr. Somers hugged us, then, looking uneasy, said he would wait for Mary Exa by the gate. Mary Exa struggled to smile. Her plump cheeks were pink, her hair was freshly swept up, and, to me, she looked lovely. It didn't matter that she'd worn the same clothes four days and nights in a row.

She had picked some white-flowered alyssum for the crown of her hat. She put a sprig through one of Edith's buttonholes, then one through mine.

"Ladies," she drawled, "I refuse to weep, because I know I shall see you both again soon. We are friends today and we shall be friends tomorrow. Only the miles separate us." Mary Exa pulled us each into a quick, tight embrace, then turned on her heels. Edith raised her hand to bid farewell, but Mary Exa had already disappeared into the crowd.

For several minutes I cried. Edith kept wiping her eyes with her sleeve. When we noticed Mr. London near the ferry landing she stretched up on her tiptoes to wave.

"Jack, hello!"

*There was no communication with the outside world
for several days. . . . Mrs. Westlake got one of her relatives who slipped
in to take several telegrams across the Bay for us and send them from
Oakland, but I heard there were over eighty-three thousand
messages on file to be sent one night.*

Chapter 27

"LOOKS LIKE YOU GALS are homeward bound," Mr. London said when he stepped onto our dock. His pants were dustier than before and his shirt was ripped.

"I'm glad we have this chance to say good-bye," he said to Edith. "The ferry's due any moment. Once across the bay, I'll board a train back to

Santa Rosa sometime today, hopefully. Here . . ."
He penciled his address on a page torn from his
notebook.

"If it's not too much trouble, please send me
some of your photographs, and do let me know if
you find your father. We could correspond."

"I'd like that," Edith said. She looked admiringly
into his blue-gray eyes as he brushed his hair off his
forehead. He turned to the sound of someone calling
him.

"Here, darling!" he called back.

Darling?

Edith's eyebrow lifted just a little. Mr. London
smiled at the pretty lady approaching us. She wore
a beige cotton dress with bell sleeves and a corseted
waist. Her auburn hair was piled neatly on her head.

He slipped his notepad into his pocket, then
draped his arm around her to make introductions.

"This is my wife, Charmian," he said proudly to
us.

Edith paled. I slipped my hand into hers to let
her know I was just as surprised as she was. Pleas-
antries were exchanged, but the light in Edith's eyes
had dimmed.

I felt silly for having thought Jack London might
marry Edith. I would never admit this to her, but

I'd even gone so far as to imagine living with them on his ranch, currying his horses, perhaps dabbling in writing and photography myself.

We listened politely while Charmian spoke of visiting her sisters, who were camped in their yard but were otherwise unharmed. Fortunately for us, a yell from the harbormaster interrupted her. Our boat was about to leave.

Edith and I pushed the buggy up the gangplank and settled onto the sunny side of the deck. My heart ached to see her wave so bravely to Mr. and Mrs. Jack London. As our boat sputtered away from the dock, sea gulls wheeled overhead, crying into the breeze.

We passed several islands in the wide, windy bay. The captain pointed to the yacht *Uarda,* a German steamer that had been safely anchored during the earthquake and fire. Its passengers had been able to watch the calamity in luxury, with plenty of wine, food, and warm feather beds.

I thought back to Wednesday morning and my first sleepy glimpse of San Francisco. Now it was Sunday. Edith stretched her legs.

"Oh, Daisy," she said. "I should have remembered he was married. I'd read it somewhere, but I

just forgot . . . what with everything turned upside
down and no sleep, Papa lost . . . Molly . . ."

"Then why didn't he mention his wife to us?"

"Maybe he was just as distracted as we were,
Daisy. Charmian London—she's beautiful, isn't
she?—she reviews books for the *Overland*. She's a
good writer. . . . I am so tired I could sleep for
days. . . . If I never wear shoes again, it'll be too
soon. Just look at us."

We were a sight. Our skirts were soiled and stiff,
our hems ragged. Our blouses, once starched white,
were gray, with dark splotches on the sleeves and
little rips in the lace. I could smell our unwashed
bodies. My scalp itched.

"It'll be at least twelve hours before we dock in
Stockton," she said. "We'll try to telephone Moke
Hill then."

I looked at Edith and felt a rush of affection. Her
long red hair and tattered clothes made her seem
pleasantly girlish. What a relief it was to be together, safe, no longer struggling inside a crowd. I
leaned over and began unlacing her shoes. Gently
I took them off. Her stockings were in bloody shreds.

"Why, Daisy, thank you." She wiggled her toes.
I undid mine, then slipped my feet free. We sat

on the smooth wood deck, warmed by the sun. Wisps of hair blew around our faces. We started to giggle.

"Are you thinking what I'm thinking?" she whispered.

Without answering, I heaved one shoe overboard, then the other. Edith did the same. I had never heard a more delighted laugh than hers.

*There has never been a correct list or estimate of
the dead published—the papers claim not over 300 and I heard it was
really thirty thousand, but I can't believe it was over 5,000.*

Chapter 28

IT WAS NEARLY MIDNIGHT when the lights of
Stockton loomed ahead. I had dozed fitfully, shiver-
ing from the damp air and the spray from the river.
Stiff and groggy, we waited for the deckhands to
rope the lines to the dock, then we pushed the buggy
up the bumpy wharf.

A team would arrive by sunup, we were told.

Telephone lines would open at 5:00 A.M., so we'd be able to leave word with Hotel Leger that we were on our way. It would take a day and a half for the horses to pull our wagon up the grade into Moke Hill.

We passed the long hours sitting on the floor of the waiting area. We were excited to be so close to home but still dreaded the news that might await us.

Edith and I shared chunks of Mrs. Somers's bread, stale as it was. I savored each bite, keeping the crust in my cheek, where it slowly dissolved.

A young boat captain slept on a bench, covered by a newspaper. I thought it odd that Edith was standing over him until I realized she was reading headlines. With disbelief on her face, she motioned me over.

" 'Death Toll in San Francisco Reaches Three Hundred,' " she quoted. *"Three hundred?* Daisy, there were half that many in just one of those boarding houses that sank." Her voice was angry as she read further. "And why is there no mention of China-town? Several *thousand* lived in Chinatown. Some may have made it to Oakland, but we only saw a few Chinese in the parks. What does this newspaper mean, only three hundred dead?"

I leaned over the man myself and even lifted one of the pages to peer on the other side.

Eventually I noticed the young captain's eyes were wide open. The shock of waking to two mussy ladies hovering over him must have been great, because he began to stutter.

"D-d-do we know each other?" he managed.

When the wagon rounded the final bend leading into Mokelumne Hill, Edith reached inside her skirt pocket. She pulled out two of Mr. Somers's lemon drops, then a rose. Its pink petals were flattened against its leaves, but its short stem was unbroken.

"Is that the one Dr. Willy gave you?"

She smiled. "It was there the whole time," she said.

The cheering that met our wagon was deafening. Buster Hornbuckle and several boys were waving their hats. Dr. Willy balanced himself on the watering trough and shaded his eyes with his hand. Mrs. Irvine stood anxiously next to Bob. Seeing her daughter alive was too much, apparently, for she swooned at Mr. Hornbuckle's feet.

When we saw Mr. Irvine running toward the wagon, Edith, overjoyed, broke into tears. "Papa!" she cried. "Papa!"

As he helped her down, I could see his eyes were wet. "Thank God you two are safe," he said, pulling her to him, then embracing me. He gazed into her face. "I searched for you, Edie, for hours and hours. I was so desperate that when someone at the harbor said he'd seen two young ladies board for Stockton—one with long red hair, if you can believe it— I took the next boat home. But you and Daisy . . . weren't here." Mr. Irvine clasped his daughter's hand, then put his other arm around me. He led us to the sidewalk, where Bob was fanning Mrs. Irvine's pale face.

"We thought you were goners," Bob said to us. "Mother nearly had a stroke, she was so heartsick." As Edith clung to her father I remembered the minister who had prayed for our safety and wished there was some way to thank him.

Everyone talked at once. Dr. Willy brazenly swept Edith into his arms, and I was amazed she let him. When she told him his sister, Tess, was safe, and the baby, too, he hugged her again. He and Edith held each other with such tenderness I was surprised.

I heard my name, but when I turned there was someone else calling from another direction. Suddenly faces blurred. I was dizzy and sick to my stomach.

A gentle hand steadied me, then helped me drink from a cool mug of sarsaparilla. When I finished, I saw the apron I was leaning into was Mr. Hornbuckle's. He looked at me so kindly I momentarily confused him with Mr. Somers.

"Mercy, we were worried," said Mrs. Hornbuckle, her immense face inches from mine. "That earthquake Wednesday morning rattled all the jars on our shelves and scared Buster's horse so bad it run off. We've been worrying ever since—about both of you, Daisy."

As soon as Pa got word I was home, he hurried to Moke Hill on horseback, much relieved to see I was suffering only from exhaustion and blistered feet; the cut on my chin, though infected, was beginning to heal.

The first week, Edith and I napped in the morning, then napped again in the afternoon. Our nights were long and wakeful. I felt hungry all the time. I found myself saving crusts of bread in my apron pockets, to suck on between meals.

I returned to the routine of dusting, polishing,

peeling potatoes, and lighting the morning stove, emptying a chamber pot now and then, and using the carpet sweeper. Charlie showed me how to starch and iron the linens. No one had asked me to do these things, but I wanted to. I wanted to earn my keep.

Also, no one said anything about our lost trip around the world. Mrs. Irvine didn't even mention the steamer trunks we had abandoned.

Neighbors dropped by with meals and polite questions. I puzzled over the abrupt changes in Mr. and Mrs. Hornbuckle, even in Mrs. Irvine. Why is it that when you're thought to be killed or missing, but it turns out you're not, people end up being nice to you?

A few days after we arrived home, the *San Francisco Chronicle* reported that the city's real-estate board had passed a resolution. From now on the phrase *Great Earthquake* was to be replaced by the phrase *Great Fire*. Folks seemed relieved to think that San Francisco's disaster was preventable: after all, better waterlines can be installed and more steam engines brought in. But an earthquake, well . . .

My words were few, Edith's fewer. How could we tell all we'd seen and the horror of it? Would they understand that we had left behind a family, that we had buried a loved one?

Mr. Irvine said even less. "City Hall is gone. All documents and claims, gone."

"What does that mean, Papa?" Edith asked.

"It means," he said, gazing out the parlor window, "financial ruin."

Two weeks after the earthquake, Mokelumne Hill celebrated May Day with a band, a picnic by the river, and a maypole dance. It was a fine spring day with a scent of lilacs and freshly mowed grass. Edith and I sat on a blanket in the sunshine, quiet, the only ladies barefoot and without hats. When Dr. Willy arrived with an armload of wild poppies, Edith smiled up at him and asked him to sit down.

That night I again had trouble sleeping. The attic windows were open, allowing the cool air to drift in. I could hear the hoot of an owl and the crickets chirping in the rosebushes. Edith was in her dark-room. This was the shed adjoining the screened porch. Something clattered to the floor and there was a heavy thump.

I leaned out the window. "Edith?" I called. When there was no response I rushed downstairs, through the dark kitchen, then outside to the shed. The dirt felt cold beneath my feet.

Light from under the door sheeted out to the yard. I knocked.

"Edith? It's Daisy." I jiggled the latch, but it was locked from inside.

I threw my weight into the door. Once. Twice. Finally it burst open.

Edith was on the floor, hugging her knees, rocking from side to side. Her mouth was open in a silent scream. Her eyes pleaded with me.

In front of her lay a photograph. I knelt beside her and picked it up. As I held it between my fingers, I felt a sob rising in my throat.

It was the horses, those magnificent white horses. She had captured them after all.

Several days later, Edith had developed sixty photos. As we studied them together, I marveled at the black-and-white images. When she had taken them, I had seen merely rocks and charred walls. She'd seen stories.

Perhaps that's why she packed up the glass plates and all her pictures—except the one of the horses. She didn't want to relive most of what she'd seen through her lens. She placed them carefully in a trunk that Charlie lifted into the attic then slid across the floor to the foot of my bed.

When she showed the photograph to her mother, Mrs. Irvine nervously fingered her brooch.

"Oh, Edith." She looked at her daughter, then she looked at me. In a flicker I knew she understood. Edith hadn't been able to tell her mother what we'd been through. Now she didn't need to.

Mrs. Irvine's face seemed thinner and more deeply creased than it was a few weeks before. The way she cast loving eyes on her daughter made me think about Clinton and the poem on his headstone.

I was glad to be home, most of all for Mrs. Irvine.

A few [street]cars were run on Sunday, two weeks after the quake—women rode free. People hailed [the streetcars] with as much delight as if they were the first ever used here. . . . We scrambled on one, rode around to see the ruins, then went to Berkeley to see the university, Greek Theater, etc.

Chapter 29

WARM AIR MOVED through the house, stirred by ceiling fans. We sat at the kitchen table, which was washed in sunlight from the south window. Mrs. Irvine poured tea for us while Edith examined the photographs Mary Exa had sent. They were torn from one of the Bay Area newspapers, and one showed the ferry building.

"I can't believe it," said Edith. "Notice anything?"

I looked at the picture. It was the ferry building,
all right. Something seemed wrong, though. Edith
hurried out to her darkroom and returned with a
magnifying glass. After a moment she passed it to
me. I could see now that an artist had doctored the
photograph to hide much of the earthquake damage.
We studied the two other pictures. I couldn't iden-
tify them, but I remembered being there.

"It's called airbrushing," Edith said. "Old pho-
tographer's trick—one I think, quite frankly, is dis-
honest, unless it's just to repair a flaw in the film.
Genthe did it with some of his Chinatown pictures.
He brushed out English signs and American-dressed
Chinese to make San Francisco seem more exotic."

Arnold Genthe was Mr. London's friend, a famous German photographer, she reminded me.
"Sometimes he hid his camera—it was a little Bae-
deker, I think—in his coat so people wouldn't shy
away. I doubt that he would have stooped to airbrushing his earthquake photos, though, if he had
been able to take any."

Edith read aloud from the magazines of yesterday's mail. Mrs. Irvine offered me the bowl of sugar.
I dropped two cubes into my cup and watched them

dissolve in the hot tea before stirring it. She set her silver spoon in her saucer, then nodded for her daughter to continue.

When Edith turned to page twenty-two of *Collier's,* she drew in her breath. She passed the large magazine across the table to me.

" 'The Story of an Eye-Witness,' " I began, " 'by Jack London' . . . *Jack London? . . . 'Collier's* Special Correspondent.' " I looked up at Edith, then continued reading. Fifteen minutes later I reached the last paragraph:

San Francisco, at the present time is like the crater of a volcano, around which are camped tens of thousands of refugees. . . . All the surrounding cities and towns are jammed with the homeless ones, where they are being cared for by the relief committees. The refugees were carried free by the railroads to any point they wished to go, and it is estimated that over one hundred thousand people have left the peninsula on which San Francisco stood.

Edith had tears in her eyes. "Good for him," she said softly. "He found the words after all."

I closed the magazine. Mrs. Irvine took the kettle

from the stove and poured steaming water into the teapot. She set out a cup for Bob, who had joined us at the table. He chuckled as he unfolded a letter from his pocket.

"Since you all are reading up a storm, here's something that'll raise your dander. It's from James Horsburgh, Junior, general passenger agent for Southern Pacific Railroad. Mr. Peek and Mr. Hornbuckle say they got this same letter; in fact it seems every chamber of commerce in California got this letter." Bob poured some of his tea into his saucer to let it cool. After slurping it up, he began to read:

"We at Southern Pacific want to set the record straight. We do not believe in advertising the earthquake. Lantern slide shows should be views only of the San Francisco that escaped earthquake damage. Show how quickly and wonderfully the state has recovered.

"The real calamity in San Francisco was undoubtedly the fire. Except for a few cities that happened to lie directly in the earthquake's path, practically no damage was done.

"Dear City Leaders, Southern Pacific stands ready to cooperate with you in every way practicable to keep California and San Francisco from being misrepresented by sensation mongers."

I looked directly at Bob. "They're *lying*," I said.

Bob chuckled again. He had the same red hair and freckled complexion as Edith, the same quick mind. "Oh, I believe you, Daisy. But this Mr. Horsburgh, Joon-yer, wants people to think that folks like you and Edith are the ones lying. Let's face it, earthquakes are bad for business."

We poor women—if the walls cracked or a window shook from a breeze we screamed "earthquake" and ran for the doors for days and days afterwards.

Chapter 30

IT WAS RAINING that night when I blew out the lamp and slid under my quilt. Bad Boy jumped onto the end of my cot, circled a few times, then settled at my feet, purring. The mulberry tree outside groaned in the wind. A branch scraped back and forth against the roof. I felt sleep wash over me.

The sudden thump of dynamite made my heart

race. I clawed at the darkness, trying not to fall from the shaking bed. *"Help,"* I cried, *"help."* There was the awful noise of glass breaking.

Someone ran in and grabbed me.

"It's all right, Daisy," said Edith. "You're all right. It's just the wind."

I let her hold me. My face pressed into the embroidered shoulder of her nightgown. She smelled of fresh soap and lilac. Her hair trailed like silk on my hand.

"A branch fell through your window. Come on." She hurried me out, then shut the attic door against the blowing rain, Bad Boy at our heels. Downstairs in her room, she unfolded an extra cot and piled it with blankets from the hall cupboard. She gave me one of her pillows.

A match flared and soon the lamp glowed, casting shadows through the cold room. Even though electricity had come to Mokelumne Hill, most of the homes still used kerosene for light. The only heat came from the kitchen stove downstairs, and that fire had gone out after supper. I shivered under blankets pulled up to my chin.

"Do you think it's raining in San Francisco?" she asked.

"I was wondering that myself."

"Daisy, it must be awful for Mary Exa and the others, living outside with no real home. I'm so glad they might come here for Christmas. . . . Oh, those poor babies and the little boys now without their mother. If only Molly . . ."

Edith fell back on her pillow, her hands over her face as she wept.

Reminded of Molly, I, too, began to cry. Outside, wind continued to bother the trees and loose shutters.

On the way back from Hornbuckle's Merchandise, I held Mrs. Irvine's parcel on my shoulder and with my free hand hiked my skirt up to my knees. Despite last night's rain, the air was pleasantly warm and held the promise of an early summer.

Unable to resist the puddles, I slopped through the wagon ruts. Mud oozed between my toes. It splattered my legs and soaked my hem. I laughed out loud. It felt good to be home.

Charlie was in the kitchen, taking a pie from the oven. "You late fo' suppa," he whispered. Mystified, I set the package down and tried to brush my sleeves clean.

"Daisy, is that you?" called a voice from the dining room. Charlie nudged me forward.

"Coming," I said, letting the door swing behind me. Mud dripped from my hem.

A cluster of candles blazed in the center of the table, which was crowded with bowls of potatoes, beets, and green beans, a plate of butter, a tureen of chili, and a basket of steaming hot cornbread. I could feel the back of my mouth begin to water.

Mr. Irvine sat at one end, Mrs. Irvine at the other. Bob was across from Edith. I noticed there was a place setting next to hers, and a vacant chair.

"Well," Edith smiled at me. "Aren't you going to sit down?"

It was a moment before I could speak. "I don't understand," I said. As their servant, I had always eaten in the kitchen with Charlie.

Mr. Irvine cleared his throat, then motioned to the empty place. "We've been having some discussions these past days, and . . . well . . . you're family now, Daisy." Without another word he began eating. Bob responded by mashing his fork into his potatoes, then pouring gravy over them.

Edith and her mother waited while I slowly pulled out the chair. It was heavy, but it made no sound on the thick carpet. When I took my napkin from its silver ring and spread it across my lap, Mrs. Irvine nodded with approval. If my dripping skirt bothered her, she didn't say so.

I wasn't sure why I now had a place at their table, but it suited me fine. My first chance to be part of a family had been my days and nights with the Popcorn Family, as Edith and I now spoke of them. It had felt so good that I was willing to try it with the Irvines.

Bob's mouth was full of bread when he looked up at me. His blue eyes were merry. "Better dig in while you can, Daisy," he said, still chewing. "That sister of mine eats like a lumberjack." He grinned at Edith, then he winked at me.

My feet were sore and blistered for two weeks afterwards, but I am quite alright again [and t]hings are looking better now, although it will take a year to clean the city. Railroads are being built in the main streets to carry off debris. . . . There are thousands of things which I have not written but do not want to overdo you in reading them. Lovingly, Mary Exa—May 1, 1906.

Afterword

The first shock on April 18, 1906, officially re-corded at 5:12:05 A.M., lasted for forty-five seconds. San Francisco's U.S. Weather Bureau recorded twenty-seven earthquakes that day. The fires, which raged for three days, and the dynamiting that was done in an effort to stop the fires, destroyed much of the evidence scientists and engineers would have needed to study structures. The damage masked an astro-nomical death toll.

The Irvines' financial loss was devastating and, as a result, they were forced to sell five of the homes they owned in town. Bob went to work building flumes near the lumber camps and, in the fall, Edith resumed teaching at Mokelumne Hill's one-room schoolhouse. Her earthquake photographs were stored in her trunk for eighty years, after which time Bob's son, James, donated them to Brigham Young University.

From 1906 to 1908, *Sunset Magagzine* paid some of the best writers and artists in the country for articles that would promote Southern Pacific Railroad's sanitized version of the disaster in San Francisco. That magazine has no relation to the present day *Sunset Magazine,* except in name.

In June of 1907 Mayor Schmitz was found guilty of graft and extortion. He spent a brief time in county jail. Despite his wish to relocate the Asian community on the outskirts of the city, away from San Francisco's choicest real estate, Chinatown was rebuilt on its original location.

Among the documents destroyed in San Francisco's City Hall were birth and immigration records. This was good news for Chinese laborers and peasants, whose families had been forbidden to enter the United States. By claiming they were U. S. citizens by birthright, the laborers were now free to send for their wives and children. The Chinese Exclusion Act of 1882 was finally repealed in 1943.

Bibliography

Andrews, Ralph W. *Photographers of the Frontier West: Their Lives and Works, 1875–1915.* Seattle: Superior Publishing Co., 1965.

Barrymore, John. *Confessions of an Actor.* Indianapolis: Bobbs-Merrill, 1926.

Bronson, William. *The Earth Shook, the Sky Burned.* Garden City, NY: Doubleday, 1959.

The Calaveras Californian. Angels Camp, CA: 1990–1991.

Campbell, Mary Exa Atkins. A letter written May 1, 1906: courtesy of Mr. and Mrs. James Atkins Tarver.

Canby, Thomas Y. "Earthquake: Prelude to the Big One?" *National Geographic.* May, 1990.

Cleland, Robert Glass. *The Irvine Ranch.* San Marino, CA: The Huntington Library, 1966.

DeLee, Joseph B., A.M., M.D. *Principles and Practices of Obstetrics.* Philadelphia: W. B. Saunders Co., 1925.

Dicker, Laverne Mau. *The Chinese in San Francisco: A Pictorial History.* New York: Dover Publications, 1979.

Dolan, Edward F., Jr. *Disaster 1906: The San Francisco Earthquake and Fire.* New York: Julian Messner, 1967.

Flagg, Michael. "Irvine Co. vs Smith." *The Los Angeles Times.* July 1, 1990.

Garst, Shannon. *Jack London: Magnet for Adventure.* New York: Julian Messner, 1963.

Genthe, Arnold; text by John Kuo Wei Tchen. *Genthe's Photographs of San Francisco's Old Chinatown.* New York: Dover Publications, 1984.

Grun, Bernard. *The Timetables of History.* New York: Simon & Schuster, 1982.

Hansen, Gladys, and Emmet Condon. *Denial of Disaster: The Untold Story and Photographs of the San Francisco Earthquake and Fire of 1906.* San Francisco: Cameron and Company, 1989.

Irvine Chamber of Commerce. Miscellaneous pamphlets, 1990.

Joy, Emmett P. *The Annals of Mokelumne Hill: The Story of a Veritable Gold Mountain.* Murphys, CA: Old Timers Museum, 1975.

London, Charmian. *The Book of Jack London.* 2 vols. New York: The Century Co., 1921.

London, Jack. "The Story of an Eye-Witness." *Collier's.* May 5, 1906.

McDowell, Jack, ed. *San Francisco.* Menlo Park, CA: Lane Publishing Co., 1986.

Moffett, Samuel E. "The Old San Francisco." *Collier's.* May 5, 1906.

Morris, Charles, ed. *The San Francisco Calamity By Earthquake and Fire, Told By Eyewitnesses.* Washington, D.C.: W. E. Scull, Library of Congress, 1906.

O'brien, Robert. "San Francisco: April 18, 1906." *Collier's.* March 30, 1956.

Palmer, Frederick. "San Francisco in Ruins." *Collier's.* May 5, 1906.

Plunket, Wilma Marie. *Edith Irvine: Her Life and Photography* (master's thesis). Brigham Young University: Provo, UT, 1989.

Saul, Eric, and Don Denevi. *The Great San Francisco Earthquake and Fire, 1906.* Millbrae, CA: Celestial Art Publishers, 1981.

Sears, Roebuck and Co. Consumers Guide. 1902 edition. New York: Crown Publishers, 1969.

Sears, Stephen W. *Hometown U.S.A.* New York: Simon & Schuster, 1982.

Thomas, Gordon, and Max Morgan Witts. *The San Francisco Earthquake.* New York: Stein & Day, 1971.

Twain, Mark. *Roughing It.* Hartford: American Publishing Co., 1872; New York: New American Library, 1962.

Zumwalt, Eve Starcevich. *The Romance of Mokelumne Hill: A Pageant of History.* Fresno, CA: Pioneer Publishing Co., 1990.

GREAT EPISODES

Other titles now available:

*Look for exciting new titles
to come in the Great Episodes
series of historical fiction.*